PATH OF TRUE LOVE

Kelly had looked after her younger sister, Amber, since their parents' deaths. Now, at eighteen, Amber has fallen in love with Michael, who is ten years older. Kelly has serious misgivings about the age difference, but she gives them her blessing when they get engaged. However, as the wedding approaches, Kelly realises that she, too, has fallen in love with Michael. She knows he is out of her reach — until one fateful day when all their lives are changed for ever . . .

MARLENE E. McFADDEN

PATH OF
TRUE LOVE

Complete and Unabridged

LINFORD
Leicester

First published in Great Britain in 2000

First Linford Edition
published 2001

British Library CIP Data

McFadden, Marlene E. (Marlene Elizabeth), *1937 –*
Path of true love.—Large print ed.—
Linford romance library
1. Love stories
2. Large type books
I. Title
813.5′4 [F]

ISBN 0–7089–9726–0

Published by
F. A. Thorpe (Publishing)
Anstey, Leicestershire

Set by Words & Graphics Ltd.
Anstey, Leicestershire
Printed and bound in Great Britain by
T. J. International Ltd., Padstow, Cornwall

This book is printed on acid-free paper

1

Kelly watched from the sitting-room window as Michael's dark blue sports car came to a stop at the head of the drive. She saw him turn to smile at Amber, then lean forward and give her a kiss on the lips. Amber said something and they both laughed as Amber removed the white scarf from her head and ran her fingers through her long hair.

She waited until Michael got out of the car and came to open the door for her, then swung her long, slender legs out and let Michael give her his hand and pull her upright. They stood very close together, looking into one another's eyes. Amber was almost as tall as Michael. Everyone said they made the perfect couple, and they did.

Kelly turned away from the window, feeling suddenly like an intruder. She

1

went through into the kitchen to put the kettle on, waiting for the burst of laughter and conversation that would herald her sister's and Michael's entrance into the house.

When Amber appeared in the kitchen doorway Kelly saw that she was armed with yet more carrier bags with such names as Harvey Nicholls and House of Fraser blazoned across them. She forced herself to smile brightly, seeing Michael come and stand behind Amber, his hands fondly on her shoulders.

'More new dresses?' Kelly said in a sisterly, teasing voice.

Amber beamed. She looked absolutely radiant. She always did, of course. She was a very beautiful girl but since she and Michael had become engaged, Amber seemed to have a sort of inner glow. Her brown eyes sparkled, her cheeks had a soft, becoming bloom. Kelly felt a sudden surge of love for this little sister of hers, seven years her junior, to whom she had been mother and sister since their parents had been killed in a road accident when she was eighteen and Amber only eleven. Now she was twenty-five, Amber eighteen and in less than a month, Amber would become Mrs Michael Hammond. It hardly seemed possible.

'This is the last of my spending, honestly, Kelly,' Amber was saying as she smiled at Michael who smiled indulgently back at her. 'I've promised, haven't I, Michael?'

'Oh, yes, you've promised,' he agreed, giving Kelly a wink. 'But you promised last week, and the week before that, if I remember rightly.'

'Now you know you don't mind,' Amber retorted.

She turned to Kelly.

'I'll just run upstairs with these. Wait till you see the dress I've bought. It's out of this world. I shall wear it for our evening reception.'

She dashed away, and Kelly knew her sister would bound up the stairs two at a time and would waltz around her bedroom. There wasn't a happier person living than Amber and since meeting and falling in love with Michael her happiness had known no bounds.

Alone in the kitchen with Michael, Kelly suddenly felt flustered. She turned to put tea bags in the pot. She heard him pull out a chair at the kitchen table and sit down.

'I can see I'm going to have my hands full with that young woman,' he remarked.

But Kelly could hear the unmistakable pride and love in his voice. He adored Amber. He was ten years older than she was and Kelly had had serious misgivings in the beginning when her sister first started going out with him. She had had casual boyfriends before, but from the very beginning Kelly sensed that her sister's relationship with Michael Hammond was very different. And she was proved to be right.

Within six months of meeting, they

had become engaged. Now just six months later they were to be married. Kelly remembered vividly the day Amber had told her of Michael's proposal. She had rushed into the house after Michael had dropped her off one night and Kelly had stared in surprise because Michael usually came in with her.

'Where's Michael?' she asked, using the remote control to switch off the television.

Amber came and sat by her on the settee, taking hold of her hand.

'Michael's asked me to marry him,' she breathed.

Kelly's heart missed a beat.

'Oh, Amber,' she said.

'Aren't you pleased?'

A fleeting shadow crossed Amber's lovely face.

'I thought you'd be over the moon. You like Michael, don't you?'

'Of course I like him,' Kelly said, smiling now, the dizzying moment passed. 'But it's a bit sudden, isn't it?

You've only just had your eighteenth birthday.'

'Yes, I know.'

Amber was dismissive about such a trivial matter as the difference in their ages.

'But we love one another so much, Kelly. Michael's such a wonderful person. He's mature and he looks after me. He's kind and gentle and generous.'

She went on extolling Michael's many virtues but Kelly scarcely heard her. All she could hear was the voice inside her head.

'I won't be able to bear it. Michael and Amber married. I thought it would blow over. Amber's so young, so immature. How can Michael want her to be his wife?' the voice kept saying.

Immediately she had thought these things she felt ashamed and quickly turned her attention back to Amber who was speaking again.

'Michael's got his own business, as you know. He's established. He doesn't want me to work after we're married and so naturally I shall be giving up my job.'

Amber hated her job, anyway. She wasn't the world's best typist and soon got bored. She had had two receptionist positions already since leaving school at sixteen. Now it seemed as though Kelly's past worries about what her sister would do in life had been for nothing. Amber would marry Michael, run their home, no doubt in time bear his children. Would that really be enough for someone with Amber's restless, often wild, spirit?

'We want your blessing, Kelly,' Amber said. 'You've practically brought me up. I wouldn't want to do anything you didn't like. That's why I sent Michael home tonight. That's why we haven't looked at any rings yet. I didn't want to until I'd told you. But I will tell you that we've already seen the house we want. Well, it's a bungalow actually. The big one on the corner of Elm Avenue, so we won't be so far away

7

from you, Kelly, darling. Michael's going to arrange for us to view it. You must come, too.'

So, in effect, it was all cut and dried, Kelly realised ruefully. She knew without a doubt that if she put her foot down, if she refused her blessing, Amber would go ahead and marry Michael anyway and she, Kelly, would lose, perhaps for ever, the love of her sister. She wouldn't let that happen.

She pulled Amber into her arms and hugged her fiercely.

'Darling, of course you have my blessing,' she cried, 'and I wouldn't dream of going along with you to view the bungalow. Not the first time you and Michael see it. It wouldn't be right.'

Amber didn't argue. She smothered Kelly with affectionate kisses and they sat into the small hours talking about weddings and honeymoons and engagement rings and Kelly tried to put out of her mind the desolation she felt knowing Michael would be beyond her reach for ever.

Now, as she poured him a cup of tea and got out the biscuit tin, she realised what a difficult task it was going to be not to love Michael. Her heart had lurched at the first sight of him, as she watched him and Amber play tennis at the village club. Kelly did not play tennis herself. She shone at no sports, but was academically very bright and was an assistant to a junior partner in a small firm of lawyers in the nearby town of Helford, who specialised in criminal law.

She had been to university, obtained a First Class Honours Law Degree and done her stint as an articled clerk. She loved her work. She had gone happily enough to the club to watch Amber play tennis with this Michael who at that point was just another of Amber's many, fleeting boyfriends.

Immediately, Kelly saw that Michael was different from any of the others. For one thing, he was so much older. For another, just seeing him, moving agilely across the court, suntanned and healthy looking in white sports shirt and shorts had set Kelly's pulse racing.

Amber had met him in Helford, at one of the two health and fitness clubs he owned, so he wasn't from the village. Kelly knew she would never have forgotten a man like that! Later, on being introduced to him, Kelly had actually found herself blushing like a schoolgirl and that night she could not sleep for thinking about him, seeing his smooth, handsome face, his fair, sun-streaked hair, those almost luminous dark eyes, his smile.

Later, her feelings settled into a dull ache of longing, something Kelly had never before experienced. She had had casual boyfriends but had never been in love. She tried to tell herself that she wasn't in love now, that Michael was Amber's boyfriend, not hers. It was hands off as far as he was concerned. None of that helped and the feeling only intensified. She had never shown by word or sign what she was feeling inside and she vowed she never would.

Now, as she heard Amber singing as she ran back downstairs, Kelly felt herself begin to relax. She was always a little tense in Michael's presence, especially if they were alone. She could only hope and pray that he was unable to detect that tension.

When Amber settled herself cosily on Michael's knee, giving him a fond kiss, saying, 'Shall we go dancing, tonight, Michael, darling?' Kelly laughed.

'Poor Michael!' she cried. 'Haven't you put him through enough for one day, dragging him all over Leeds?'

'Thank you, Kelly,' Michael acknowledged, 'for those few words of moral support.'

Amber groaned.

'Yes, yes, yes, we will go dancing,' she said, sounding cross, probably half serious and half joking, because Amber liked to get her own way.

Michael sighed and shrugged his shoulders.

'What can a man do?' he moaned,

but Kelly knew he was loving every minute of it.

In his eyes, Amber could do no wrong. He spoiled her, but then hadn't she herself always spoiled her sister, never saying no to her, trying to make up, she supposed, for them not having any parents. Michael would take over where Kelly left off. Yes, they would go dancing till the small hours and tomorrow, a Sunday, they would go horse riding together. They were never happier than when indulging in some sport or another. They were a golden couple and they would make a fairytale bride and groom, Kelly thought, with yet another wince of inner sadness and pain.

The next few weeks seemed to fly by. Amber floated on a cloud and it was left to Kelly to keep her own feet firmly on the ground so that she could supervise all the arrangements, attend to matters that could only be done virtually at the last minute and be the substitute mother for her sister she had always been in the past.

Wedding presents were arriving almost daily now and were arranged on the dining-room table, which they rarely used. Amber loved the presents and insisted on arranging them all herself, making sure each card was attached to the right gift. She spent a great deal of time simply looking at everything like an excited child on Christmas morning.

Kelly could not help wondering, the nearer it got to the wedding day, how Amber would cope with running her own home. She was not in the least domesticated and made no secret of the fact that she hated cooking. Once, when Michael had teased her about her lack of culinary skills, Amber had said, 'You'll have to get me a cook/ housekeeper, Michael, darling.'

Michael had replied placidly, 'I might just do that, angel.'

One way or another, Kelly knew, her little sister would always come up smiling.

Four days before the wedding came the time for hair appointments and manicures, for the last fitting of the wedding and bridesmaids' dresses and the final once-over of the table seating plans. Also, for praying that the beautiful June weather would continue. Wasn't it said that a girl who married in June would always remain a bride?

The wedding was to take place at the village church of St Mark at two o'clock on Saturday afternoon. At just after midnight on the Thursday before, Kelly and Amber were awoken by a frantic knocking at the door. Amber appeared in Kelly's bedroom doorway as she was struggling into her dressing-gown. Amber's eyes were wild and scared, her hair was loose around her shoulders.

'Who is it, do you think?' she asked in a hoarse whisper.

'I don't know,' Kelly said, trying to keep her voice steady.

They went downstairs together. The front door was a solid one with a circular pane of patterned glass in the top half through which could be seen two figures. With her heart in her mouth Kelly unlocked and opened the door whilst Amber hovered at her shoulder.

Outside stood Mr and Mrs Hammond. Michael's father had his arm around his wife's shoulder. Kelly could see the collar of his striped pyjamas showing under his hurriedly thrown-on jacket. Her heart contracted and she heard Amber let out a long, low moan.

Mrs Hammond burst into tears and before Kelly could say a word she cried, 'Oh, Kelly, there's been the most dreadful accident. We couldn't phone. We couldn't let poor Amber learn over the phone. It's Michael.'

She broke off, covering her face with her hands, sobbing in anguish.

Kelly ushered Michael's parents into the hall. Amber had started to cry, loud, hysterical sobs. Kelly forced herself to keep calm, unable to ask the question to which she dreaded to hear the answer.

2

They waited in the little room at the hospital for news of Michael's condition. Information about the accident had been sketchily provided by Mr and Mrs Hammond who were only able to relate what the police had already told them.

'Michael's sports car collided with another car on his way home from Karl's,' Mr Hammond said. 'The other driver was over the alcohol limit, and we know no more than that. He got away with just cuts and bruises. Whilst Michael . . . oh . . . '

He rubbed his hand across his eyes.

After her first hysterical outburst Amber had gone uncharacteristically quiet. Her face was deathly pale, her eyes seeming larger than ever. She kept twisting her engagement ring round and round. After Mr Hammond had

16

spoken she spoke in a loud, flat-sounding voice.

'I should have been with Michael tonight. We'd both been invited to Karl's and Carol's for a meal, but I had forgotten and arranged to go out with Julie instead. I'm like that, aren't I, scatter-brained and forgetful. Michael always teases me about it. He says I'll probably forget to go to church on Saturday.'

She paused and looked at Kelly.

'But then we won't be getting married on Saturday, will we? Karl was Michael's best man, you know.'

Mr Hammond spoke again.

'Karl said Michael hadn't touched a drop. Sober as a judge, he said. But that's Michael, isn't it? He doesn't drink much at the best of times. Never when he's driving. Isn't that right, Amber?'

Amber nodded.

'Yes, that's right. His car's a write-off, you say? Michael loved that car.'

Kelly felt so helpless. She didn't

know what to say or do to give the Hammonds and Amber any comfort or hope, if there was any hope to give, of course. They didn't yet know the extent of Michael's injuries except that, after immediate medical attention in the casualty department, he'd been admitted to the intensive care unit.

The situation felt unreal to Kelly. She must be in a state of shock, she realised, still numb and unbelieving. She stared at the half-empty polystyrene cups of coffee on the waiting-room table. It would be cold now. Why were they taking such a long time? Surely they knew by now how things were with Michael. Surely someone could spare a minute to come along and talk to them.

Mrs Hammond was sobbing quietly in a controlled, somehow dignified manner. Amber wasn't doing anything but sitting there, staring straight ahead, breathing in short, harsh breaths as though she had just been jogging. Kelly herself was feeling her heart beginning to break as she faced the possibility that

18

Michael might die. She suddenly wanted to be sick. She stood up abruptly.

'What is it?' Mr Hammond asked sharply.

'Nothing. I need to go to the bathroom,' she managed to say.

She started for the door but before she could open it a young, Asian doctor in a white coat appeared in the corridor and entered the waiting-room. His face was solemn. Mr Hammond got to his feet. Both Amber and Mrs Hammond remained seated.

'Well, Doctor?' Mr Hammond said.

'Well, your son's suffered some serious injuries, Mr Hammond,' the doctor began in a quiet, well-educated voice. 'His left leg is badly mangled and his left wrist is broken. He's got various cuts and bruises and a very badly-gashed face. Most of his injuries will heal very well with time, but we're rather worried about the leg. We're doing all we can.'

'Is he going to live, doctor?' Mr

Hammond asked the all-important question, and in response the young doctor gave a faint but definite smile.

'Oh, yes, he's out of any immediate danger. There doesn't appear to be any internal injuries and no head injuries apart from the facial lacerations.'

For the first time, Mr Hammond started to weep, tears coursing down his cheeks.

'Thank God!' he murmured. 'Do you hear that, Amy? Michael's going to be all right.'

Perhaps he sounded too joyous; perhaps the young doctor believed he himself had sounded over-optimistic. He started to speak.

'Please, remember, Mr Hammond, there's a long, hard road ahead of your son,' but none of them was really listening.

Michael was going to live! That's all anyone wanted to know just then.

They let them go in to see Michael after that, but only in pairs. Generously,

Mrs Hammond pushed Amber forward.

'You go first, Amber, with Kelly,' she said.

'No, you must go with Amber,' Kelly returned, knowing it was the right thing to do though she was desperate to see Michael for herself.

Mrs Hammond shook her head, giving a faint smile.

'You take Amber. It's all right, Kelly.'

Kelly didn't argue further. She felt Amber's fingers digging into her arm as they walked along the corridor and through the swing doors towards where Michael was lying. Neither of them was prepared for what they saw. Amber's tears came at last and she collapsed into a chair by the bed, taking hold of Michael's good hand, bending over it, her tears already wetting the bed covers.

'Michael, oh, Michael!' she wept helplessly.

His face was a mass of dressings, one eye almost shut but he was conscious and his lips twisted into an anguished smile.

'Don't cry, angel,' he whispered, his voice scarcely audible, but his words only made Amber cry the more.

Kelly took a chair on the other side of the bed. There was a cage over Michael's left leg and his left arm was in plaster. He was linked up to a heart monitor and a drip. He looked a mess and Kelly wanted nothing more than to take him in her arms and let her own tears drip on to him, but she sat there and watched Michael feebly attempt to stroke Amber's hair and listened to him whispering endearments to her.

Kelly felt she ought to go out of the room and leave them alone together. It was obvious even now when he was so badly injured and no doubt in pain and disorientated that Michael was more concerned with Amber's well-being than his own. To see the expression of such love was humbling but also heart-rending because Kelly knew she herself would never, ever stop loving this man.

★ ★ ★

Amber took another look around the room that would be Michael's for the time being. It was on the ground floor of the Hammonds' home, with a large bay window overlooking the long, back garden. There would be comfort and privacy for a man who, the doctors had informed them, would be in a wheel-chair for some time to come.

'We haven't forgotten anything, have we, Kelly?' Amber asked, looking anxiously at her sister.

Kelly smiled.

'I'm sure we haven't,' she said.

She felt sometimes to be in the way, as though she should be leaving Amber and Mrs Hammond, the fiancée and mother of Michael, to make their arrangements and plans together, but Amber had insisted on having her there, today of all days, when Michael

23

was coming home.

Amber was restless and nervous, checking the most minor details over and over. Kelly knew it was hard for her. She should by rights be Michael's wife now, wearing his wedding ring, bearing his name, sharing his home, not twisting her hands together, her face wet from tears she had shed earlier.

'I don't know how I shall cope,' she stammered, going to look out into the sunlit garden.

Kelly joined her, putting her arm around her sister.

'You'll be fine,' she comforted.

Amber was to move in with the Hammonds for a while, so that she and Michael could be near one another. When Michael had suggested they hire a nurse to tend to his needs his mother had looked horrified.

'Of course not, Michael,' she protested. 'Amber will want to do that, won't you, Amber? And I'll help, you know I will.'

Michael had fallen silent as his

mother went on at some length about their plans to turn the small breakfast room into a bedsitting room for him. Kelly, who, on Amber's insistence, was visiting the hospital with them had watched Michael's impassive face.

He doesn't like this, she thought. He doesn't want to be helpless in front of either Amber or his mother.

'Luckily,' Mrs Hammond had chattered on, 'we have a downstairs bathroom so there'll be no problems there, but your father is going to have some minor adjustments made. Don't worry, darling, we'll cope just fine.'

Kelly knew Mrs Hammond was only trying to sound optimistic, but she was overdoing it. The more she said, the more Michael seemed to shrivel up.

Amber, as was usual in Michael's presence, said very little. She was finding it very hard to come to terms, not only with the knowledge that he would be crippled in one leg for the rest of his life, but with the permanent facial scars that no amount of surgery would put right entirely. At the moment these scars were particularly livid, one dark red gash slicing across Michael's right cheek, another smaller one over one eyebrow.

He had been told there would be more healing, but on the other hand no-one had tried to pull the wool over his eyes.

Now, in the room where he would sleep, if he could sleep that was, Kelly could not stop worrying that he might lie in that narrow bed simply staring at the ceiling. Amber began to voice her fears.

'Michael won't ever be the same again, will he, Kelly?' she said, not turning from staring blankly across the garden. 'I know he won't be confined to a wheel-chair for the rest of his life, but he's not going to be able to do the things he did before the accident, his swimming, tennis, jogging . . . '

Her voice trailed off.

'Oh, I'm sure he'll be able to swim,' Kelly said reassuringly. 'Even people who are paralysed can swim, you know.'

'But that won't be enough.'

Amber sounded angry as she swung round to face her sister.

'Not for Michael, and not for me. Michael's whole life revolves around being fit and keeping fit. How can he run his health clubs now? He won't be a very good advertisement, moving about in a wheel-chair or using a stick and that's what it will amount to, isn't it?'

Kelly felt a surge of anger.

'Amber, don't talk like that! How can you sound so cruel?'

But Amber hadn't finished. Taking two steps into the room she continued.

'And his face, his beautiful face.'

Her own face crumpled and she put her hands over it and sobbed helplessly so that Kelly did not hesitate to draw her sister gently into her arms again.

'I know it's awful, Amber,' she said, 'but you mustn't let Michael see you so upset. I've noticed when we're visiting you hardly talk to him. In fact, you hardly look at him. He's not a fool, Amber. And why don't you want to see him by yourself? Why do you always insist I'm there, or Mrs Hammond?'

Amber pulled free.

'Because I'm so frightened, that's why. I don't know what to say to him.'

'Then you're going to have to start forgetting about yourself, about your own feelings and think of Michael. You're going to be his wife. I'm sure as soon as he's able to walk down the aisle Michael will want the wedding to go ahead, so you can move into your bungalow and get on with your lives. Surely that's what you want as well.'

She paused and when Amber didn't speak she added, 'Isn't it?'

Amber flushed and looked down at her feet.

'I don't know,' she mumbled.

Kelly stared at her sister, aghast. She couldn't believe what she was hearing. But then, mingled with the horror, she experienced a small upward surge of hope. If Amber jilted Michael . . .

She quickly flung out that callous, wicked thought. To deflect the anger she felt away from herself, she turned it on Amber. She grabbed her sister by the shoulders and shook her viciously.

'Of course, it's what you want. You love Michael and he loves you, and he needs you. He needs your love and support, for better or for worse, remember.'

'I haven't made any vows yet,' Amber reminded her and worse than the words that she was uttering was the coolness with which she did so.

Despite her own feelings for Michael, or perhaps because of them, Kelly knew she had to make Amber realise how badly she was behaving and how she would hate herself afterwards.

'You're not a child, Amber,' she said, speaking calmly now, gently. 'And Michael is just the same man as he ever was. He's coming home today. Put yourself in his place. Don't you think he's going to feel terrible? Guilty even for what's happened to him?'

29

Amber frowned.

'Why should he feel guilty? The accident was in no way Michael's fault.'

'Not because of the accident, because of what he's done to you,' Kelly tried to explain.

Amber went and sat on the edge of the bed.

'I don't understand,' she said. 'What has Michael done to me?'

'Directly, nothing, but trying to think how Michael will feel, I'm sure he'll have convinced himself by now that he's hurt you badly. You were less than three days from your wedding. You had all your life before you. Michael had shown how well he was going to be able to provide for you, to care for you and protect you. Now, well, for the time being he's helpless and reliant on you, not you on him. How must that feel to a man like Michael?'

Kelly sat down by her sister on the bed and took hold of her fingers. They were icy cold despite the warm, sunny day.

'Amber, now is the time for you to be the strong one,' Kelly said.

She said no more. They sat silently for several moments until tears welled once more into Amber's tawny eyes. Her lips trembled.

'I'm sorry, Kelly,' she began. 'I'm so sorry. I didn't realise how selfish I was. I love Michael very much, please, don't ever doubt that. I'll look after him, I'll help him regain his strength and when we're married I'll be the best wife a man ever had. I promise you.'

They hugged one another. As Kelly looked over Amber's shoulder, her eyes fixed on the pattern of white daisies on the wallpaper, she tried to feel overjoyed that she had managed to convince her sister of where her duty lay. But would duty be enough? Would Amber's declared love for Michael be enough? There were tough times ahead.

Kelly knew one thing for certain. After the wedding, she would put the house on the market and move away from this village where she had been born and lived all her life. She would go right away from Helford. It was the only way, for Amber, Michael and for herself.

3

On the day that Michael cast aside his wheel-chair for good, he insisted on celebrating by throwing a small party for family and close friends, not at his parents' house, but at the bungalow he and Amber were to share when they were married.

Kelly was delighted when she received her invitation. She had not seen either Amber or Michael for some time, deliberately keeping a low profile, allowing them time to adjust to Michael's new condition. She had not even phoned Amber very much and did not let her sister know that she had kept in close touch with Mrs Hammond to see how things were going.

Now, she walked round to Elm Avenue, crunching through the fallen autumn leaves along the pavement. How rapidly the time had passed. Soon winter would be upon them. Amber and Michael had not, so far as Kelly knew, set a new date for their wedding, but surely it would be soon. Then Kelly would be able to put her own plan into action and try to sell the house. This was her secret for the time being.

Outside the bungalow, she paused. There was a long, straight drive, set between neat gardens. The bungalow was stone built with lattice-paned windows. How fortunate, Kelly thought, that Amber and Michael had chosen a one-storey house. It couldn't have been more fortuitous. There were a couple of cars already parked in the driveway. Mr and Mrs Hammond's was one of them.

Kelly knew she was facing quite an ordeal. Every encounter with Michael made her realise more and more how much he meant to her and how unattainable he was. As she paused at the end of the drive, Amber came and looked out of the window. She saw Kelly and waved frantically and by the time Kelly had reached the front door,

Amber had opened it and was ushering her inside.

'Come in, come in,' she urged.

Kelly stepped inside the wide hall from where doors opened on either side. This was only the second time she had been to the house and the first time had been soon after Michael and Amber bought it when it was still unfurnished. She saw at once that the hall, at least, had been newly decorated and carpeted in a warm, rich burgundy carpet.

'Everything looks so new,' she remarked, somewhat foolishly, she realised immediately.

'Everything is new,' Amber declared.

Kelly studied her sister. She looked very lovely today in a straight-skirted black dress whose darkness was effectively relieved with crisp white collar and cuffs, giving the dress a sort of puritan look, but despite her bright chatter, her eagerness to show off her soon-to-be-home, Kelly did not miss the dark smudges under Amber's eyes, nor the pallor of her cheeks, despite the carefully-applied make up.

As Amber made to open the door to the sitting-room from where a murmur of voices could be heard, Kelly caught hold of her arm.

'Is everything all right, Amber?' she asked.

'Of course. Why shouldn't it be? Isn't it exciting that Michael can say goodbye to his chair once and for all?'

'Wonderful!' Kelly agreed heartily.

Amber opened the door with a flourish.

'Here's Kelly!' she cried.

There were five people already in the room — Michael's parents and Karl and Carol Chesters. Karl had been Michael's best friend since their school-days and was due to officiate as his best man when he got married. Mr Hammond and Karl got to their feet as soon as Kelly appeared, but Michael was already standing, leaning heavily on a stick. He had his back to the fireplace at the far end of the large, square room.

Kelly hardly noticed the furniture, the rich, wall-to-wall carpeting, the pictures on the walls. Her eyes took in only Michael's appearance. He seemed to have lost weight. His face was definitely thinner and the livid scar stood out across his cheek, but when he smiled at Kelly, she knew that this was still the same Michael. No scars or disability could ever change him.

He started to walk towards her and she could see it was a tremendous effort for him and wondered briefly if he had not abandoned his wheel-chair rather prematurely. But his expression was one of grim determination and she admired him for his courage. He reached her side and leaned forward to kiss her cheek. The touch of his lips was like a mild, electric shock.

'Kelly, how are you?' he asked.

'Shouldn't I be asking you that question, Michael?' Kelly replied.

Michael waved his hand airily.

'Oh, I'm fine, on top of the world, aren't I, darling?'

He held out his free hand to Amber and she came and stood close by him, resting her head against him. She gave Kelly a tremulous smile.

'I don't want Michael to try to run before he can walk,' she said quietly.

Michael gave her shoulders a little shake.

'I know my limitations, angel, believe me,' he said, and Kelly thought she detected a slight edge to his voice.

Had there been tension between them? The next moment, Michael was asking Amber to pour Kelly a glass of champagne.

'Champagne?'

Kelly's eyebrows rose.

'Of course. What else would we be drinking? I walked round the block this afternoon. Next week I'm going down to the club. Got to keep my hand in, you know, or my colleagues might run my business into the ground.'

He was teasing. Kelly knew that Michael had an excellent relationship with every member of staff who helped to run his health and fitness centres and that he trusted them implicitly.

Soon the other invited guests arrived. The sitting-room was so spacious that it almost swallowed them up. Kelly made polite conversation with the Hammonds, who were so proud of their son's achievements and had nothing but praise for Amber.

'She's going to make Michael a wonderful wife,' Mrs Hammond said.

'It hasn't been easy for her, you know,' Mr Hammond remarked. 'She's so young, so full of life. Of course, so is Michael, or he was.'

He said the last words with an obvious tinge of sadness in his voice, and Mrs Hammond looked shocked.

'John, you mustn't think like that,' she scolded her husband. 'Michael would be most upset if he heard you. You know how hard he's trying. He's told us he's going to the club, and mark my words, before this year is over he'll be doing all the things he did before the accident.'

Did she really believe that, or was she just trying to convince herself? Was that brave optimism Mrs Hammond's way of dealing with the situation? Kelly saw Michael going out of the room. Why, oh, why, wouldn't he sit down? Why did he insist on keeping on his feet? The strain was beginning to tell on him. To her eyes at least, his limp was becoming more and more pronounced as the afternoon progressed. Kelly glanced at Amber but she was busy chatting to Carol Chesters.

Relieved when she noticed the next door neighbour, an elderly widow who had been kindly keeping an eye on the bungalow whilst it was empty, coming to talk to the Hammonds, Kelly excused herself and went in search of Michael. He was in the kitchen, and he was sitting down, gulping a glass of water.

'Gosh, that tasted good,' he said, smiling at Kelly as she stood in the open kitchen doorway.

'May I join you?' she asked.

Michael waved his glass airily.

'Be my guest,' he said.

'I'll give the water a miss, but I'll sit down, if I may.'

Kelly sat at the other end of the long, scrubbed pine table. The kitchen was enormous. From outside, the bungalow didn't look particularly big, but all the rooms were spacious. She noticed the small brown pill bottle in front of Michael.

'Are you in pain?' she asked gently.

He grimaced.

'You could say that,' he confessed. 'Not to worry. These little blighters will soon do the trick. But don't you dare go telling Amber that I'm taking painkillers.'

'Don't you think she has a right to know, Michael?' Kelly asked.

'To blazes with rights. I don't want her worrying about me. She's gone through too much already.'

'I won't tell her,' Kelly promised.

Michael relaxed, grinning. When his lips twitched up in a smile, the scar

41

seemed to crease, giving Michael's face a rather lop-sided appearance. It was strange, but at that moment Kelly could not for the life of her remember exactly how Michael had looked before the scar. To her, it had already become a part of him, something to love, like the gentleness of his eyes, the nuances of his voice.

'There's one good thing about this place,' Michael said, seeming to change the subject.

'What's that?'

'No stairs.'

'It's a beautiful house,' Kelly said.

'Yes, I know. Amber loves it. I shall be glad when we're finally married and have moved in here together. I'm toying with the idea of moving in anyway, by myself, now that I'm mobile.'

It was on the tip of Kelly's tongue to ask if he really thought he'd be able to manage alone, but she bit back the words. Of course he would manage. She must get rid of the idea that Michael was some sort of invalid. She felt ashamed she had even considered asking the question.

'Actually,' Michael began and started twisting the pill bottle in his hands, not looking at her, 'I wondered if it might be appropriate to make the announcement today.'

'What announcement?' Kelly asked.

He looked at her then.

'About the wedding. Amber doesn't know it yet, but I've been to see the vicar of St Mark's and I've provisionally fixed a new date. I've also checked with the restaurant where we're going to have the reception, and the evening disco. I think enough time's gone by, don't you?'

He looked down at his outstretched leg, prodding it gently with his stick.

'What's the point in waiting any longer? Perhaps this is going to be as good as it gets.'

'I think it's something you should discuss with Amber in private, Michael,' Kelly told him, 'before you make any sort of announcement.'

She was surprised when once again he gave her the lop-sided grin.

'I'd a feeling that's what you'd say,' he remarked.

He used the stick to push himself to his feet.

'Well, let's get back to the others. The pills have worked, for a few hours anyway.'

He moved off in front of her as though suddenly eager to get back to Amber's side. Kelly sat at the table for a few moments longer, staring at the empty glass on the table where Michael had been sitting.

It was only a matter of time now till Michael and Amber were married. As Michael had just said, what was the point in waiting any longer? Suddenly the anticipated upheaval in her own life seemed to loom alarmingly close and for the first time Kelly had grave doubts that she would be able to put her plans into action.

4

Apart from the light left burning in the hall, the house was in darkness when Kelly arrived home from work about a week later. Both she and Amber always left the hall light on when the house was unoccupied after dark, so Kelly presumed Amber was with Michael.

True to his word, he had moved into the bungalow and Amber spent most of her spare time with him. Kelly let herself in, hung her coat in the hallrobe, picked up the couple of letters from the hall mat and went through into the kitchen. Thank goodness for central heating, she thought. The weather had turned very chilly and the welcoming warmth of the house was pleasant.

As the kitchen flooded with light, Kelly saw the white envelope propped against the coffee jar on the work surface. Her name was scrawled across the front in Amber's untidy handwriting. Still totally unaware of what awaited her, Kelly switched on the kettle to make a cup of tea and sat down at the kitchen table. She tore open the envelope and unfolded the single sheet of paper and started to read.

Dear Kelly, I know I'm being a coward not telling you face to face, but this was the only way I could do it. I've told Michael we're finished. I can't go through with the wedding. Please, don't hate me, Kelly. It just wouldn't be right for me to marry Michael feeling the way I do. I know I'm a cruel, terrible person and no-one can hate me as much as I hate myself. I can't face you or Michael's parents so I'm going away.

At the moment I don't know where I shall finish up, but please don't worry about me. I'm a big girl now and I can look after myself. I have my building society account book and I can get another reception position. I handed in my notice, by the way. I didn't just leave them in the lurch. When everything and everybody has calmed down and I'm settled somewhere I'll be in touch. I love you, Kelly. Lots of love, Amber.

And that was it — brief, to the point. Yet Amber had given no reasons for her terrible decision. Had she been more forthcoming with Michael?

The kettle switched itself off but Kelly did not move from the table, still holding the letter in her hand, feeling as though a block of ice had formed around her heart. She and Amber had never been apart, except for holidays and most of them they had spent together. Where had she gone? What would she do? Frustration and anger began to melt the chilling ice a little.

How could she? Yes, Amber was a coward, a coward of the worst kind, and her behaviour left Kelly wondering seriously if her sister had ever really loved Michael, or had she simply been in love with love, falling for the handsome, outdoor type of man Michael had been because his characteristics and his looks fitted Amber's image of what an ideal man should be?

Now that Michael, in Amber's eyes, was marred, her love for him had disappeared like early-morning mist before the sun and she would rather leave her home and her job, everything she knew and held dear, than become Michael's wife.

Once again Kelly's emotions altered. Michael! What must he be feeling? Was he alone at the bungalow? Had he called his parents? He was very close to them, but he was a very proud man. The way he was handling himself since his accident showed that.

Kelly didn't know what to do. Should she phone him? Should she go round there? And what could she say or do if she did? As she sat there the shrill ringing of the telephone made her jump. Her mouth went suddenly dry as she went into the hall to answer it. It was Michael and Kelly wasn't surprised to hear his voice. He spoke sharply.

'Is Amber there?'

'No, she's gone, Michael. She's left me a note.'

There was no point in hiding the truth from him.

'She didn't waste much time, did she?' he said bitterly. 'She only told me today. I couldn't believe it, not at first, until I stopped kidding myself and realised the writing had been on the wall ever since the accident. Amber didn't want to be lumbered with a cripple. She made that pretty obvious.'

Kelly cringed at the description he was applying to himself.

'Surely Amber didn't say anything so terrible,' she said.

'Not in so many words, no, but she doesn't want to marry me, so doesn't that speak for itself? When are you expecting her back?'

So he didn't know Amber had gone away for good.

'I'm not, Michael,' she said as gently as she could. 'That's what the note was about. Amber's gone for good.'

'Gone where?'

'I don't know. She didn't say. To tell you the truth I don't think she knows herself, but she says she won't be coming back. Not for the foreseeable future anyway.'

'I thought I might be able to talk some sense into her.'

The anger had gone from Michael's voice. He sounded weary and infinitely sad. Kelly's heart went out to him.

'I'm sorry, Michael,' she said and felt the tears starting to prick the back of her eyes. 'Have you told your parents?'

'I've told no-one but you, Kelly. They'll have to know sooner or later, I realise that, but I can't face them just yet, especially not my mother. She'll be round here like a shot, weeping and making endless cups of tea. I can't take that. Oh, Kelly, I don't know what I'll do without Amber.'

His voice had broken. Kelly desperately wanted to comfort him but didn't know how to. She felt distanced from him on the end of the phone. Then she knew that he was crying and she knew she had to go to him.

'Michael, shall I come round?' she asked.

'What can you do? What can anybody do?' Michael sobbed.

It was heart-rending to hear a man crying. He shouldn't be alone.

'Not a great deal,' Kelly confessed, 'but I'll be someone to talk to, at least, and I promise not to weep or make endless cups of tea.'

He gave a half-hearted laugh.

'Fair enough,' he said.

Kelly hadn't had anything to eat since lunch time and it was now nearly seven o'clock, but she had a feeling Michael wouldn't have eaten either. If she made something for herself perhaps she could persuade him to eat some-thing as well.

'I'll come straight away,' she said and replaced the receiver quickly before Michael could tell her not to go.

She got her coat out again and this

time she took the car for the short journey to Elm Avenue. She wanted to be there as quickly as she could. A light showed through the curtains of the sitting-room as Kelly parked in the drive and went to ring the doorbell.

Michael answered it, leaning on his stick. There was no sign of the tears she had heard down the phone, but he looked as weary as he had sounded and his usually well-groomed hair was untidy as though he had been running his fingers through it. The love she felt for him swelled up inside Kelly. She knew she shouldn't feel that way. She knew that at this time above any other she must be what Michael needed most — a good friend.

'Thanks for coming, Kelly,' Michael greeted her.

He took her into the sitting-room. It was cosy and warm. There was a cheery fire burning in the redbrick hearth.

'The fire looks lovely,' Kelly remarked removing her coat and moving to sit in one of the comfortable armchairs.

'We've taken to lighting it now the evenings are getting colder,' Michael said, taking Kelly's coat. 'Having a real fire was Amber's idea. Not that I minded, of course, but now . . . it's a bit of a fuss . . . a bit messy. I don't think I'll bother again.'

Kelly didn't argue. She liked the look of a real fire, too, but for convenience she had one of the more modern gas ones that gave the appearance of an open fire. Michael took her coat into the hall and came and stood in the doorway.

'Can I get you something to drink?' he asked.

'Not just now, later. I thought I might rustle us up something to eat. I'm willing to bet you haven't bothered cooking anything for yourself.'

Michael gave a faint smile.

'You're right, I haven't.'

'And I've missed my supper,' Kelly told him.

Michael came and sat in the chair opposite her, stretching out his leg, wincing as he did, so that Kelly knew he was still suffering some pain from his injuries.

'I'm sorry I've kept you from your meal, Kelly,' he apologised.

He propped his stick against the side of the fireplace.

'It doesn't matter,' she said.

There was a silence, during which the fire crackled and shifted. Under other circumstances Kelly would have leaned back her head, closed her eyes and listened to the noises of the fire, feeling the warmth and comfort of the room surrounding her, soothing her. Now she looked at her hands, feeling awkward. The silence had an emptiness about it simply because Amber, bubbly, bouncy Amber, wasn't there and neither of them knew where she was.

As if reading her thoughts, Michael said, 'What are we going to do about Amber then?'

Kelly looked at him. He was trying to

54

sound cheerful, but there was pain in his eyes that wasn't caused by his wounds and for a moment Kelly's anger against her sister surged anew.

'What can we do, Michael?' she asked plaintively.

'I know what I'd like to do,' Michael said angrily. 'I'd like to wring her beautiful neck. That would give me intense pleasure right now.'

'Join the club,' Kelly said.

'Seriously, can you tell me what I can do with the rest of my life? I'm blowed if I can see straight just at the moment.'

The anger had gone and Michael rubbed his hand across his eyes, his head bent forward. Kelly wanted to go to him but she stayed where she was, trying to think of something useful to say. What did you say in a situation like this? Kelly had certainly never experienced anything like it in her own life.

True, Amber herself had had boyfriends who had left her and she had even wept tears over one or two of them and declared that her life was over, but she had always bounced back. This was different. Not only had Amber made it plain she didn't love Michael but had left him in no doubt as to why she no longer wanted to marry him.

Michael went on without waiting for an answer to his question.

'And how do I go about letting everybody know? Karl and Carol, all our other friends. My mother and father! I can only thank God that I didn't re-book the wedding reception. But there are the presents. Do they all have to be sent back?'

She didn't care about the presents, and yet she knew Michael was right. Practicalities had to be considered. People would need to be told. Suddenly the list of things that had to be done seemed endless. And on top of all this, Michael was still attending physio-therapy sessions at the hospital and perhaps facing the possibility of plastic surgery on his face. How could he cope with it all?

Kelly's own troubles were as nothing

compared to Michael's. Her sister had gone missing, but she knew that Amber, whatever her other faults, was capable of looking after herself. She might not have ever had any driving ambition to carve out a career for herself, but now she might be different, now her circumstances had changed so drastically.

'It suddenly seems,' Michael said, 'as though my whole life has come to an end. We had everything, Amber and I. Perhaps we were too happy. Do you think that's possible? Do you think we tried to take too much from life and didn't give anything back? Do you think I'm being punished, Kelly, for being too full of myself, too self-centred?'

'Stop it, stop it!'

Kelly stood up and walked over to Michael's chair.

'Don't talk like that.'

She couldn't let him go on blaming himself in that manner. Nothing could be further from the truth than what Michael was thinking about himself at that moment. His feelings were understandable but he had to snap out of it. She saw that now, otherwise he would go on wallowing in grief, and if he did, Kelly knew it would severely set back his progress towards physical recovery.

He would never be exactly the man he had been before the accident. No-one knew that and accepted it better than Michael himself, but he had to be able to believe in himself, to fight, not to give in. Oh, how dearly Kelly wanted to say, 'She's not worth it, Michael. She's my sister and I love her, but she's really not worth what you're doing to yourself.'

She knew she couldn't of course, but she knew she had to be strong and she prayed for the strength in herself that would help him to get through this.

5

Let's go for a drink,' Michael said grimly as they left the court buildings, causing his mother to frown.

'Do you think that's wise, Michael?' she asked.

'Wise or not, Mother, I need a drink,' Michael insisted and limped off down the court steps.

His parents and Kelly followed on behind. They all three knew better than to try to assist Michael down the steps. Kelly saw the worried look on Mrs Hammond's face and put her hand on the other woman's arm.

'Don't worry, Mrs Hammond,' she said. 'I'll look after Michael. I'll drive him home and I'll only be drinking orange juice.'

Mrs Hammond gave Kelly an uncertain smile.

'Well, if you're sure. Poor Michael. I

know he didn't like the verdict. Did any of us? A fine and twelve months' driving ban! That man ruined my son's life and he gets away with it.'

She was getting upset and Mr Hammond put his arm around her.

'It was a very hefty fine, Amy,' he reminded her gently.

Kelly didn't think it was the right moment to mention that Michael would be able to sue for damages against the driver who had maimed him. She, too, thought the punishment was too lenient. She only hoped that having to come to court, having to go over all that had happened, would not set Michael back. He had been doing so well, going to his health centres, taking an interest in his work again, and beginning to take an interest in his life after Amber's departure.

It was now December and neither of them had heard a word from Amber, not a letter, not a phone call. Kelly prayed every night that her sister was safe and well and repeatedly told herself that no news was good news.

As for Michael, he never mentioned Amber. It was as though he had never known and loved her. But in his unguarded moments Kelly could see by his expression that he still cared for her, still missed her. As for herself, if anything, her feelings for Michael had grown even stronger, but they still remained her closely-guarded secret. She had resigned herself to believing it would always be so.

Kelly chatted to Mr and Mrs Hammond for a few moments before hurrying along to catch up with Michael. He was waiting in the car park by Kelly's car. Michael had still not taken up driving again and generally used taxis wherever he went, except that today he had asked Kelly to go to court with him.

There was no way she would have refused him, so she had taken a day off work and told Mr and Mrs Hammond that there was no point in their driving over from Helford to pick up Michael.

It was a bitterly cold day with a strong, north wind but Michael was standing there with his top coat unbuttoned. His face looked pinched and cold. Kelly hurried to unlock the car door and release the catch of the passenger door so Michael could get in. She had set the seat as far back as she could but still Michael's long legs seemed squashed. His stick, which he still used, and which Kelly knew he hated, was propped between his legs.

He didn't look at her as he said, 'Well, where to, Kelly?'

Kelly rarely went into any public house in Helford. Even in the village, in a cosy, olde worlde pub like the Fox and Grapes, she was not a frequent customer, but she knew it would be quiet there at this time of day and that there would be a log fire burning.

'Let's go to the Fox and Grapes, shall we?' she suggested. 'It won't take us long.'

Michael nodded.

As they drove along, Michael said,

'Do you know, I hoped I might feel better after today. Vengeance is sweet and all that, but I don't feel anything but cheated. I just wonder what that chap would have got if I'd been killed. A year or two, do you think?'

Kelly concentrated on her driving.

'I don't know, Michael,' she said honestly.

Michael stared at her.

'What? You don't have any opinion and you a lawyer!'

'But I'm not a magistrate,' she said.

'Not even a custodial sentence of any kind,' Michael went on.

When he banged his hand down on the dashboard it made Kelly jump. She had spent so long helping Michael to come to terms not only with his disability but with the loss of Amber, she couldn't bear it if he descended into bitterness and self-pity again.

'Try to put it out of your mind, Michael,' she told him. 'I know that won't be easy. I know it isn't over yet. I know, too, how you must feel, but you've got to look forward not backwards. Don't I keep telling you that?'

He was silent for a long time and Kelly began to wonder if she had said too much. Did she harp on too much and too often about stiff upper lips and squared shoulders? She had never considered herself to be a chivvying sort of person. There were times, even now, when she wanted to take Michael in her arms and comfort him after all he had gone through.

Today, if she could have stood face to face with the young, rather arrogant driver of the other car in Michael's crash, she could cheerfully have spat in his face, but such conduct would not have helped anybody, least of all Michael.

When Michael spoke she detected an ironic, half-joking note in his voice.

'After Amber left, you picked me up off the floor, dusted me down and dried my tears. I'll never forget what you did for me, Kelly. You've been a real friend. When I was beginning to sink under a sea of pity and over-protectiveness, not only from my mother but from practically everybody else, you were there, quietly urging me to get on with my life and I thank you for that. I'm not going to let you down now, Kelly.

'I haven't told you yet but I've arranged for a private physiotherapist to work on my leg. Oh, the hospital was fine, but I felt so much the invalid when I went there, seeing so many others, some like myself, some who were much worse, of course. This fellow is going to come to the house three times a week. He's actively encouraging me to take up exercise at the gym again, and to go swimming. And there's more. I've seen a plastic surgeon who seems pretty confident they can do something with my face.'

He suddenly grinned at her and, seeing that grin, a weight seemed to be lifted from Kelly's shoulders.

'Who knows, I might end up looking like Mel Gibson or some such person. Wouldn't that be something?'

Kelly laughed. They were approaching the Fox and Grapes by then. It was the first time in many weeks that Michael had referred to Amber and he had dropped her name so casually into the conversation. That in itself was a good sign. The court case was out of the way. Michael, it seemed, was thinking very positively about his life. Things could only get better.

'I tell you what,' she said, sweeping into a convenient parking place in front of the pub. 'Why don't you buy me lunch? I'm just ready for one of their homemade steak and kidney pies.'

'You're on,' Michael said.

* * *

It really did seem to be a new beginning in their lives. Whenever they met, Kelly could see that Michael's energy knew no bounds. He positively threw himself into every activity he was capable of, and some that he wasn't, pushing himself to the very limits. Kelly knew he was still having pain in his leg and that occasionally he had to rely on painkillers, but the new physiotherapist was working wonders and Michael's leg was improving steadily.

It was just a few days before Christmas when Michael phoned Kelly at work and asked her to go out for a meal with him that evening. They hadn't eaten out since the day of the court case. Kelly had been extremely busy at work and Michael, of course, had very little free time. When they did meet it was usually at one another's homes, or they sometimes went to the Fox and Grapes for a drink.

This evening, Michael said when he phoned, 'It's a special occasion, Kelly, a pre-Christmas celebration if you like. You can't turn me down. I've already booked a table at that new Italian restaurant in Helford.'

Kelly had no intention of turning him down. They arranged that Michael would send a taxi round to Kelly's place at eight o'clock, having first been picked up himself. When Kelly protested and said she could pick Michael up in her car, he answered firmly.

'I wouldn't hear of it. We're doing it in style. Eight o'clock sharp then?'

She didn't argue any further.

She had a long, leisurely bath when she got home, washing and blow drying her long, fair hair. She did her nails and applied her make-up with care, finally putting on a new dress she had bought that afternoon.

When she was ready, she studied her image in the mirror in her bedroom. The dress was sleek, black and expensive and with it she wore the single string of real pearls that had been her mother's. For some reason as she looked herself she was reminded of the day she went round to the bungalow in Elm Avenue and Amber was wearing a black dress and looking particularly beautiful.

That day had been a celebration, too, the occasion when Michael had abandoned his wheel-chair for good. He had been so happy, so looking forward to being able to set another date for the wedding. But Kelly also remembered the moment she and Michael had spent together in the kitchen, when she first became aware how much pain he was suffering. She had wanted to love and comfort him then. Now she knew they could only ever be friends. There was never a hint of anything more between them. Just to be near him was enough for her.

On the dot of eight, the doorbell rang. Kelly got her coat, slipping it on as she went to answer the door. It was Michael who stood there and parked outside on the road was a dark-coloured car which was certainly not a taxi.

'Your chariot awaits, madam,' Michael said, with a sweeping bow.

'Are you driving, Michael?' Kelly asked, coming out and locking the door behind her.

'I am,' he said. 'That gleaming car in elegant racing green is my new acquisition. And that's not all.'

He lifted up his arms.

'Do you notice anything different about me?'

Under the light of the outside lamp she studied him. Was he wearing a new shirt perhaps? Had he had his hair cut recently? But, no. To Kelly, Michael looked exactly the same. If he could have detected the wild beating of her heart at the very sight of him, she was sure he would be very surprised.

'Look at my hands, woman!' he cried in mock impatience.

She looked and understanding dawned.

'No stick!' she exclaimed, smiling.

'Exactly. No stick. Now watch me walk to the car unaided.'

The limp was still there, probably always would be, but Michael was walking without his stick, and to Kelly that was a small miracle. She watched him walk the length of the drive to the car and when he turned triumphantly to look at her she ran towards him and threw her arms around his neck.

'Oh, Michael, that's wonderful!' she cried.

'I knew you'd be pleased,' Michael said, beaming. 'You're the first person to know.'

Still in his arms, Kelly looked up into his eyes. He looked radiant and Kelly desperately wanted to say, 'I love you, Michael,' but she held the words back. She couldn't risk upsetting Michael, hurting him. Just because he never mentioned Amber did not mean he had stopped loving her. She was sure he hadn't.

Then suddenly, standing there, close together in the cold, night air, Michael bent towards her and kissed her lips. There was nothing passionate in the kiss and it was over almost as soon as it had begun. Then Michael released her.

'Merry Christmas, Kelly,' he said softly.

He was making light of the kiss, she knew that, but her lips were tingling and if he hadn't been there she would have put her fingers against her mouth, as though to hold the kiss there for ever.

Kelly was glad that that brief moment of intimacy did not mar the evening. The meal was excellent. Almost every table was occupied, but the atmosphere was quiet and subdued. The conversation between Michael and Kelly was light. From the outset Michael had said there would be no talk of injuries or of how well he was doing.

'We're just two friends enjoying a meal together,' he insisted.

Just two friends? Of course they were. Michael was right. Kelly amused him with stories about some of her work colleagues. She told him of the annual office Christmas party where the usual people got up to the usual antics. Neither of them mentioned Amber though she was very much in Kelly's thoughts. After all, Christmas was less than a week away now. It would be the first Christmas the two sisters had spent apart. Where was Amber? What sort of Christmas was she planning? So far there had not been so much as a card from her.

As they were waiting for their coffee, Michael said, 'By the way, you're coming to us for Christmas Day lunch. My mother insists on it. I'm sorry I haven't mentioned it earlier. Mother thinks I issued her invitation weeks ago so don't tell her I haven't or she won't be very pleased with me.'

Kelly laughed.

'I'd love to come,' she said. 'At your parents' house, I presume?'

'Oh, yes, and don't eat anything for at least two days beforehand or you'll never manage all my mother puts before you.'

Kelly liked Michael's parents very much but did have some misgivings about going to them on Christmas Day. She was sure that Mrs Hammond, by her very nature, would not be able to resist mentioning Amber. After all, Amber would have been their daughter-in-law. Kelly and Michael had both carefully avoided mentioning her. But Christmas, above all other times, was an occasion for remembering absent friends. How hard would it be to keep from upsetting Michael? Kelly knew he still had raw wounds about the girl he had loved so much.

It was only then, when the evening was almost over, that Michael, as though tuning in to what Kelly was thinking said, 'You haven't heard anything from Amber, have you, Kelly?'

His sudden question surprised her. She shook her head.

'No, nothing.'

'Do you think she's all right?'

He sounded worried.

'It's strange, isn't it, that she hasn't contacted you by now? I can understand why she wouldn't write or phone me, but you're her sister.'

Because he was voicing Kelly's own thoughts, she felt her stomach muscles tighten with tension. It certainly wasn't like Amber.

'I do worry sometimes,' she admitted.

'I wonder at times what I'd feel like if I saw her again, I must admit,' Michael said, smiling ruefully at Kelly. 'Perhaps its for the best that she hasn't come back home. Let sleeping dogs lie, eh?'

Kelly didn't know what to say. A serious note had entered their conversation. Kelly was glad when the young waiter arrived with their coffee and Michael asked for the bill. Not long after that he took her home.

As he drew up outside Kelly's house she was once again reminded of how he had kissed her and she felt a little apprehensive, sure that Michael would also remember the moment, but the kiss was not repeated. Michael insisted on walking her to the door and waiting till she'd opened it. She toyed with the idea of asking him in for a coffee, but it was late and she was going to court tomorrow morning. She still had some notes to go over before she went to bed.

Michael stamped his feet and rubbed

his gloved hands together.

'Gosh, it's raw,' he gasped. 'You'd better get inside before you freeze to death. I'll give you a call tomorrow, shall I?'

'Yes, do, and thank you, Michael, for a wonderful evening.'

Michael smiled. 'My pleasure,' he said.

She watched him walk back to his car. The limp seemed more pronounced somehow as though perhaps he had overdone the time without his stick, though she was sure Michael would have no intention of ever using it again. Before he drove off, he waved to her and she waved back, then stood watching till his tail lights disappeared at the end of the street.

Inside the hall, she leaned against the wall, feeling suddenly very much alone. No Amber, no Michael. Amber may return one day and all would be forgiven if not forgotten, but at that moment, Kelly was convinced Michael would never be hers. They could be friends. He was no doubt very fond of her in a sisterly way, but she was sure it went no further than that and just then she wondered if she could handle that knowledge and live with it.

6

It snowed a little on Christmas Eve, starting in the middle of the afternoon and Kelly left the office early, along with everybody else. The Christmas greetings of her colleagues echoed in her ears as she set off home, knowing her Christmas would be much quieter than anybody else's.

She had never been one for clubs and pubs and that in itself did not worry her, but being alone in the house all over Christmas did. True, there would be the lunch at the Hammonds' the next day and her neighbour had invited her in for sherry and mince pies on Boxing Day morning, but that would not take care of the long, lonely evenings.

If only Michael had come forward with an invitation of some sort, that would have made Kelly's Christmas, but he hadn't, and she could not help wondering if the reason he wasn't planning much celebrating himself was because of Amber. Amber was absent in body but very much in Kelly's mind. Wasn't it understandable that Michael, too, should be pre-occupied with the girl who should have been his wife?

The soft white flakes fell silently as Kelly garaged her car and walked towards the front door. She hoped there wouldn't be too heavy a fall. She didn't particularly relish shovelling it away on Christmas morning.

As she closed the door behind her, she noticed that the few items of post, mostly Christmas cards by the look of it, were on the hall table, not lying behind the door. She also noticed the appetising smell of cooking food drifting on the air. Was Michael here? But how could he be — he didn't have a key. Only Amber, besides herself, had a key! As Kelly moved quickly through the hall, the kitchen door opened and her sister stood there.

'Amber!' Kelly cried, so happy and relieved to see her.

They hugged one another.

'I'm cooking a casserole,' Amber said. 'I've been here since this morning. I thought it would be nice for you to have a meal ready when you came home, but you're a bit early. I'm afraid it won't be ready for about another hour at least.'

Kelly removed her coat.

'That doesn't matter. Oh, Amber, it's so good to see you. I've been so worried about you. How did you get here?'

'A friend of mine brought me. I am learning to drive now so I shall have my own transport as soon as I've passed my test.'

'That's good. Come into the sitting-room. Let's have a drink.'

The gas fire had been lit, the curtains drawn and the room was warm and seemed to envelop Kelly after the cold outside. She put on a couple of lamps. How good it felt to have Amber there again after so long coming home to an empty house.

'I haven't come to stay,' Amber said. 'Holly, my friend, is coming back for me later.'

'But you must stay, Amber,' Kelly protested. 'It's snowing. You can't leave tonight, especially on Christmas Eve.'

Even as she spoke, she was wondering what Michael would think if she turned up tomorrow with Amber in tow. Amber shook her head.

'No, I'll be all right. I honestly can't stay. It wouldn't be fair. Holly's my flat mate. She's got some relatives in Helford, as it happens, and we shan't be leaving late.'

Kelly poured two glasses of sherry.

'But where are you living, Amber? I want to know everything that's happened to you.'

Amber gave a little laugh.

'Not a great deal, really. I've living in York.'

Kelly stared at her.

'York!' she repeated.

'I went there straight away. I don't know why, but it didn't seem like a long way to go. Holly was advertising for a flatmate and we seemed to get on like a house on fire straight away, so that was that. I'm working, of course, another reception job. But in the New Year, I'm starting an evening course doing my GCSEs and if I do well, I shall try for university.'

She had spoken fast and now sounded rather breathless. Kelly looked at her in amazement.

'So you haven't let the grass grow under your feet, have you?'

'I thought it was high time I did something with my life. I've flitted about up to now doing nothing in particular,' Amber replied rather shyly.

'But you were going to get married. I wouldn't call that exactly doing nothing,' Kelly reminded her.

When she saw the expression on Amber's face, she wished she could unsay the words. Amber looked stricken. The next moment, Kelly was glad they would now be able to talk about Michael. There was no point in putting off the inevitable.

'How is Michael?' Amber asked quietly.

'He's fine. He walks without a stick now.'

'Was he very upset when I left?'

Kelly couldn't lie.

'Yes,' she said simply.

'I expect he hates me.'

Amber's voice had a note of resignation.

'No, of course he doesn't. Time heals all wounds, you know.'

It was a platitude but Kelly could not think of anything else to say. Part of her wanted to try to urge Amber to change her mind about staying, but another part held a niggling worry that if she did, if Amber and Michael met again after being apart for so long, and now that Michael was so much improved, might they not rekindle their love for one another — a love that Kelly was sure, on Michael's part at least, had never really died.

She felt a deep self-loathing at that

moment. She should be doing all in her power to try to bring Amber and Michael together again, but she couldn't be so noble, not then when Amber had more or less dropped out of the heavens so abruptly. But why, she suddenly wondered, had Amber come home like she had without any warning.

She heard herself asking this question out loud. Amber twirled the sherry glass in her long, slender fingers.

'Well, it's Christmas. I wanted to see you. I've kept meaning to write, or phone, but I always held back. Then last night, when Holly told me she was visiting Helford, I decided on the spur of the moment to come with her. I'm sorry, Kelly, for the trouble I've caused, for worrying you.'

'But you're here now, aren't you, so that's all that matters.'

Amber looked at her.

'But I won't be seeing Michael,' she said firmly. 'Nothing has changed and I wouldn't want Michael upset again. If he's getting over me, and I'm glad you say he is, there's no point in hurting him all over again.'

Kelly knew she had never said Michael was getting over Amber but she did not correct her sister.

'So you won't stay even for one night?' she asked.

'No, I can't.'

Amber stood up and went out into the hall, returning with a gaily wrapped parcel which she held out towards Kelly.

'I've brought you a present. Shall I put it under the tree?'

'Yes, please. Your present's upstairs. I'll give it to you before you go. I'm so glad you're here, Amber.'

Amber came and kissed her.

'And don't worry about me, please. I'm doing all right.'

'You must keep in touch. Promise me you will?'

'I promise,' Amber said. 'I'll give you my address and phone number before I leave. Now, I'd better look at that casserole. Don't expect too much. My cooking skills aren't any better than they used to be.'

'I could eat a horse.' Kelly grinned.

'Oh, I think the casserole will taste a little bit better than that,' Amber teased and on that light note they both moved off into the kitchen.

The snow had stopped by the time Amber's friend, Holly, came to collect her and there was only a very light covering. They sky was clear and star-filled. Holly seemed a nice person, perhaps a couple of years older than Amber, with a mass of red curls, freckles and a bright and bubbly manner. Amber told her Holly was already at university, reading physics and chemistry. Kelly watched them leave, sorry to see Amber going, holding back the sudden rush of foolish tears as she waved after the departing car.

She closed the door against the cold of the night and went to start the washing up. Now, of course, she must decide whether or not to tell Michael that Amber had been to the house. She deliberated long and hard about what would be the best thing to do, but by the time she went to bed she still had not made up her mind.

★ ★ ★

Christmas Day began with a very traditional cold and frosty morning. Kelly opened her presents. Amber had bought her a silver pendant and chain in an unusual, modern design. There were things like perfume and handkerchiefs from people at the office. Her boss had given her an enormous box of expensive Belgian chocolates and a book token. Mrs Landis, the neighbour who had invited Kelly on Boxing Day morning, had bought a fluffy bright red scarf.

As yet, there was no gift from either Michael or the Hammonds, but Kelly expected there would be when she went round for lunch. She very much wanted to see Michael again. It seemed ages since they had met, but she was nervous, too, because in a strange way she felt that Amber would be there, standing between them.

Kelly made her own way to the Hammonds as Michael had stayed over there on Christmas Eve. He had wanted to collect her but she wouldn't hear of it. Michael, understandably, might want a drink on Christmas Day and wouldn't be able to have one if he had to ferry her backwards and forwards. Mr and Mrs Hammond welcomed her to their home with affectionate kisses and greetings. Michael also kissed her but only as his parents had done, lightly, on the cheek.

He looked very well and very handsome in a pale grey shirt under a darker grey sweater. There was a log fire burning in the sitting-room and a huge Christmas tree with red, blue and silver fairy lights in one corner. Kelly looked round at all the Christmas cards which seemed to adorn every surface and were also strung on coloured ribbons along the walls.

'There must be dozens,' she said.

Amy Hammond smiled.

'I've almost run out of places to put them.'

She urged Kelly to sit down and Mr Hammond offered her sherry but, because she would be driving, she settled for a soft drink.

'Of course,' Mrs Hammond went on wistfully, 'I was dearly hoping we might get a card from Amber, but we didn't.'

Now was Kelly's opportunity to speak up, but she kept silent. Even if she decided to tell about Amber's visit to the house, she would want to first tell Michael on his own.

After what seemed an awkward pause Michael said cheerfully, 'Now, open your presents, Kelly.'

He passed her the last two parcels that were nestling under the tree. She handled them excitedly, her fingers running over their intriguing shapes. She loved opening Christmas presents. She loved everything about Christmas, the tree, the decorations, Christmas pudding, mince pies, the air of happiness and friendliness that seemed to affect almost everyone.

Of course, Christmas was also the time for families and friends to get together. Often it was the only time of the year when they did, so this year there was a hollowness caused by Amber's absence, but Kelly was grateful for the short while she had been able to spend with her sister and the knowledge that Amber was all right.

She opened the Hammonds' present first. It was a beautiful paperweight of Caithness glass. Kelly smoothed her fingers over its surface.

'Thank you, it's lovely,' she said, putting it carefully back in its tissue-lined box.

'We didn't know what to get you,' Mrs Hammond said.

'You couldn't have picked anything nicer,' Kelly assured her.

Michael's gift was soft and much larger. There was no way of telling what it contained and for some reason Kelly felt a little reticent about opening it.

'Go on, it won't bite,' Michael said, smiling at her from his chair near the roaring fire.

Kelly undid the red ribbon and tore back the holly-patterned wrapping paper, revealing a soft tan leather shoulder bag. She looked at Michael.

'Thank you, Michael,' she said, feeling inwardly emotional.

'My pleasure,' he said. 'Actually I got tired of seeing you always toting that huge black thing everywhere you go.'

So he had noticed the voluminous bag she normally carried. It was a necessary evil in her work, of course, but she did tend to take it with her everywhere. Now she wouldn't have to. She'd even brought it with her today! From it she extracted the presents she herself had brought — a pair of golfing gloves for Mr Hammond, knowing his passion for the game, some pretty Austrian crystal earrings for Michael's mother and for Michael himself a day-to-a-page leather-bound desk diary.

She knew it was functional, if not to say boring, but she hadn't known what else to choose because she was afraid to buy him anything too personal. Maybe it was silly of her, but that's how she felt. At any rate, he seemed pleased with it.

As the day progressed, it became obvious that Kelly was not going to get much of an opportunity to talk to Michael alone and as she would be driving herself home there would be no chance then either. Mr and Mrs Hammond were charming hosts but always there, eager to please. However, Kelly did notice how happy and relaxed Michael looked. How could she risk spoiling his happiness by telling him about Amber's visit?

After the remark made by Mrs Hammond about a Christmas card, Amber's name was never mentioned again until she and Kelly were alone in the kitchen, washing up after lunch. Kelly had insisted, against great protestation from Mrs Hammond, in helping with this formidable task.

Michael's mother did not look at Kelly as she remarked in a casual voice, 'I wonder what Amber is doing just at this moment.'

Kelly felt her cheeks flushing rather guiltily knowing what she did.

'I expect she's celebrating Christmas with the new friends she's bound to have made,' she said, hoping her words would make it sound as though Amber was sure to be having a wonderful time without a care in the world.

'Well, she is very young. I suppose we shouldn't begrudge her happiness. When she left Michael so cruelly like she did, I thought I would never be able to forgive her, but I'm finding I can. I can see how much improved Michael is. He's happy again now and I thought he never would be. I'm so proud of the progress he's made.'

'I think we all are,' Kelly said softly.

Mrs Hammond pulled out the plug and wiped her soapy hands on a small towel. She leaned against the sink, looking at Kelly.

'He's very fond of you, Kelly,' she said, almost shyly, as though believing she shouldn't be making such a remark.

'And I'm fond of him.'

Kelly could feel her heart thumping and hoped Mrs Hammond wouldn't be able to detect it. Mrs Hammond smiled slowly.

'Ah, but you're meaning fond as a sister-in-law would have been, aren't you? I'm not. Perhaps I shouldn't say this, Kelly, but now I do really begin to wonder if Amber and Michael breaking up wasn't for the best. Oh, don't get me wrong. I don't mean I'm glad Michael had that terrible accident. Of course not. I wouldn't wish that on my worst enemy, but they do say good things often come out of bad, and well, Amber is so much younger than Michael. I can't help wondering if any marriage between them might not have been a happy one. Does that sound awful, Kelly? I don't mean it to.'

Poor Mrs Hammond was getting

flustered. Kelly wanted to reassure her but knew she had to choose her words carefully.

'I know what you're trying to say, Mrs Hammond,' she began, 'and I understand how you feel, but, as for Michael and me, we're just friends, trite though that may sound. Amber is my sister and I couldn't . . . '

She broke off, looking away.

Mrs Hammond put a gentle hand on her arm.

'Of course you couldn't, dear. Forget I ever said anything.'

She bustled about the kitchen, wiping the work surfaces unnecessarily with a damp cloth.

But how could Kelly forget when she loved Michael so much? To think what Mrs Hammond had said might be true, that Michael was fond of her, gave her a sharp pang of bitter-sweetness, an aching yearning for what might have been if circumstances had been different, if she and not Amber had first met Michael Hammond.

7

Several weeks later, when Kelly answered the phone and heard Michael's voice she could tell at once that he was very excited.

'Can I come round this evening?' he asked. 'If you've nothing planned, of course.'

She hadn't. She had brought some papers home from the office to go over, but she could easily put that job off if there was any opportunity of being with Michael.

'Yes, come round,' she said. 'But what's the matter? You sound on top of the world.'

'Wait till I see you,' Michael said darkly.

It was now nearly the end of January and the threat of snow just before Christmas had remained just that, at least in their part of the world. There had been no further visit from Amber though they had phoned one another occasionally, Kelly always eager to know that Amber was well.

So far, Kelly had not told Michael anything. She kept assuring herself that should Michael ever enquire about Amber, show the slightest curiosity about her, she would tell him all she knew, and always carefully avoided listening to the stabs of her conscience which told her he had a right to know that Amber had been in touch.

When Michael arrived, Kelly ushered him into the sitting-room and offered to go and make some coffee, but Michael caught hold of her arm and pulled her down on to the sofa beside him.

'Coffee can wait, Kelly,' he said, smiling. 'I haven't come for coffee.'

'Then why have you come?' Kelly asked.

Sitting so close to him, looking into his intense, dark eyes, she found herself wishing the answer to that question was that Michael had something important to say about the two of them; that he had fallen in love with her; that he had had an earth-shattering moment when he had realised without a doubt that she was the only woman in the world for him.

But she knew she was dreaming and she pulled herself together, waiting for Michael to speak.

'First, I've been to see that consultant plastic surgeon, the one I told you about. He's almost completely certain that he can do something about this.'

Michael touched the scar on his face lightly. It was still quite livid and had changed Michael's face for ever, but he had accepted it. As for Kelly, to her Michael was unchanged. How often did she long to be able to smooth her fingers over his face, to kiss his scar, to whisper that she loved him and would do so for the rest of her life?

Before she could tell him how pleased she was at his news, Michael went on, 'He's going to try to schedule the operation for early spring, April or

May perhaps. I'm going privately, by the way, that's why there won't be any delay. Of course, I'm never going to look the way I did before the accident, I realise that.'

Kelly caught hold of his hand and gave it a squeeze. She couldn't help it.

'It'll be fine, Michael,' she said.

'So you think I'm doing the right thing, do you?'

'Of course. Go for it!'

He squeezed her hand in return.

'I knew I could rely on your support. My parents, especially my mother, are having some misgivings about it. Mum thinks I should leave well alone now. She thinks I've been through enough and she also thinks if the operation doesn't make the scar vanish completely, I'll be disappointed, which is nonsense. I know it won't do that, I'm not a fool.'

Michael certainly wasn't a fool. He was incredibly brave and Kelly loved him all the more because of it.

Michael took a deep breath and went

on, 'And now for the really important news.'

'You mean there's more?'

What else could he have to tell her that was as important as what he had just said? Michael nodded.

'I've also been in touch with my solicitor and it seems more than highly probable that I'll be offered substantial damages because of the accident. Well, I've decided what I'm going to do with them. In fact, I can't wait for any settlement there might or might not be, so I'm going ahead anyway.'

'Going ahead with what?'

Kelly could hardly contain her curiosity. It seemed to her that Michael was taking a long time to get to the point.

'I've decided I'm going to have the health and fitness centres adapted to cater more for disabled clients. It's something that should have been done when I started them, I realise that now, but better late than never. I've acquired the services of a good architect, who happens to be a wheel-chair user himself, following a car accident, so he's more than qualified to prepare any plans that might be needed. Don't you think so?'

Now that Michael had started talking about this new project of his, Kelly could see at once how dear to his heart it was. She thought it was a brilliant idea and told him so.

He began to tick off on his fingers the modifications he had planned.

'There'll be specially-adapted equipment and showers, of course. And I'm thinking about having a hydrotherapy pool installed, and there'll be access ramps everywhere. It won't come cheap, any of it, but I'm determined. I shall have to engage the services of specially-trained helpers. Philip, my architect, has already told me he intends to enrol as my first new member.'

At last Michael paused, looking at her in a half-hesitant way.

'I'm sorry,' he apologised with a

smile. 'I know I tend to go on a bit, but I'm just so excited.'

Kelly could see that. By now Michael's enthusiasm was beginning to rub off on her. This was just what he needed — a new dimension in his life, a new goal to aim for, especially with the prospect of another operation looming on the horizon. Kelly remembered those terrible dark days after the accident when it was not even known whether Michael would walk again.

She remembered Michael's despair when Amber left him, and now here he was, less than twelve months later, fully mobile, living his life to the full. She had no doubt that come summer he would be back once more on the tennis court and taking part in all his favourite sports. Perhaps it wouldn't be with his pre-accident agility, but certainly to the best of his ability.

Unhappily, Kelly knew she would not be joining him in his activities. Her few attempts to wield a tennis racket had been pathetic, and that was when she was a schoolgirl. She could swim, and quite enjoyed it, but that was the extent of her prowess as a sportswoman and she couldn't see there being a miraculous improvement now.

Amber was the person who had always been Michael's equal, sometimes even his superior. Sports had occupied a great deal of their time together. Kelly was still not sure about telling Michael about Amber being back in touch, but decided not to spoil his excitement over his new project. He had something now to focus on, and the time would come when he was more able to face the possibility of seeing Amber again — something Kelly dreaded. Would her friendship with Michael, which she now depended on, come under threat once again?

She stood up abruptly. While Amber was completely out of Michael's life there might or might not be a chance for Kelly, an outside chance, but there all the same.

'I'll make that coffee now, Michael,'

she said, trying to keep her voice as light as possible.

As she went into the kitchen, she felt her excitement at all Michael had told her start to drain away, to be replaced with unhappiness and guilt. He mustn't see how she felt. She must simply be there for him, as and when he needed her. There was nothing else she could do.

When she went back into the sitting-room with the coffee, Michael was busy scribbling on a piece of paper, resting on a magazine on his lap.

'I've pinched the paper from your bureau,' he said, looking up at her.

'What are you doing?' Kelly asked, setting the tray down on the coffee table beside him.

'Oh, just making a few notes, scribbling the odd sketch.'

'Is it private, or may I take a look?'

Michael seemed surprised Kelly should ask such a question.

'Nothing's secret from you, Kelly,' he said. 'I want you with me every step of the way in this.'

He held the paper towards her.

'Not that you'll be able to make head or tail of what I've done. I'm no designer.'

Kelly looked at the haphazard sketches. He was right. Nothing made much sense to her. She couldn't even read Michael's handwriting!

'You're a terrible writer,' she told him.

He grinned.

'Aren't I just?' he replied.

Kelly handed him his coffee mug.

'Feel free to make any suggestions you want. Believe me, I shall welcome them,' he told her.

Kelly was pleased and proud that Michael wanted to include her in his new project, though at this stage she didn't feel there was a great deal she could offer. However, Michael did not stop at merely showing her these preliminary sketches.

He phoned her every evening if there were any new developments to inform her of. Whenever she could make it, he took her along to meet Philip Conrad, the young, disabled architect, to whom she took an instant liking. Like Michael, he was a man of great energy and verve who had adapted to life in a wheel-chair with incredible determination.

One evening, Michael took Kelly to the same Italian restaurant they had visited just before Christmas. Kelly was vividly reminded of how Michael had kissed her that evening and wondered if he, too, had remembered. Whilst they ate, Michael brought up another subject concerning his fitness centres.

'I'm thinking of re-naming them,' he began, 'and re-decorating. Might as well go the whole hog.'

'But I rather like the names you have already,' Kelly said.

Michael looked doubtful.

'Too obvious,' he remarked. 'Too lacking in imagination. Prime Fitness I and Prime Fitness II. I have a hunch that some people might be put off by such names.'

'But you have a very strong membership at both clubs, don't you?' Kelly asked.

'Oh, yes, I can't grumble, but now that I'm planning to make all my facilities available to people who, let's face it, aren't in prime fitness, I think those names are rather tactless.'

Michael picked up his knife and fork and attacked his newly-arrived main course with gusto.

'So, come on, Kelly, get your thinking cap on, there's a good girl.'

She laughed.

'You want something that projects a softer image, do you?' she asked.

'Yes, I suppose I do,' Michael agreed.

'Well, if you're going to re-decorate, why not have a particular colour scheme and re-name each centre with its individual colour scheme?'

Michael thought for a moment, then said, 'Like Crimson Palace for example?'

'No! That's terrible,' Kelly cried. 'That sounds more like a nightclub and a lurid one at that. I was thinking of something more relaxing, more soothing.'

Michael laughed.

'We don't want people to fall asleep, you know,' he said.

She ignored him.

'I rather like the colour cinnamon,' she said, 'and I even like the word cinnamon. How about something like Cinnamon Place?'

'Cinnamon Place,' Michael repeated thoughtfully. 'Yes, I think I like that. Cinnamon Place, with the decor in shades of cinnamon and white. That's great. And the other centre?'

Carried away now, Kelly said, 'Peppermint Place with mint green and white decor?'

She was surprised when Michael got out of his seat and in full view of the other diners, came and kissed her on the lips.

'You should go into public relations,

Kelly,' he praised her. 'You're wasted practising law.'

Kelly flushed and hoped the subdued lights wouldn't give her away. She remained on cloud nine for the rest of the evening, whilst Michael seemed to talk of nothing but his future plans.

When he dropped her off outside the house he said softly, 'Have I been the most incredible bore tonight, Kelly?'

She hurriedly shook her head.

'Oh, no, not at all.'

'Well, all I can say is you're a wonderful listener.'

'That's because I'm interested, Michael,' Kelly said simply.

'Are you really?'

His eyes looked solemnly into hers.

'Yes, of course.'

'Are you interested in me, too?'

Kelly didn't know what to say to that. She looked down at her hands.

'May I come in for a coffee?' Michael asked.

This was an unusual request. They always finished off their meal with coffee at the restaurant and Michael would then drive straight home. Tonight, though she didn't want coffee, Kelly did want Michael to come into the house. She felt her nerves become taut. It was as though she was waiting in anticipation for something to happen, something tremendous.

'Yes, come in, please,' she said.

They walked silently up the drive, but once inside the hall with the door closed, Michael did not hesitate. He pulled Kelly into his arms and kissed her long and deeply. The rough tweed of Michael's overcoat brushed against Kelly's flushed face. When the kiss ended he still held her tenderly in his arms.

'You don't know how much or how often I've wanted to do that,' he murmured.

'Oh, Michael!' were the only words Kelly could find to say.

'I'm in love with you. I think I've been in love with you for quite some time. I've never dared tell you because I was afraid the feeling wasn't returned. But tonight, seeing you there, with your eyes so bright and shining, I knew I couldn't hold back any longer. Oh, Kelly, is there any hope for me, do you think?'

She pulled away from him with a little laugh.

'Let's go into the sitting-room,' she said.

'No, not until you answer my question. I'm not budging until then.'

'Of course I love you, Michael,' Kelly breathed.

He kissed her again and then he allowed her to remove his top coat and helped her off with her own. Kelly's heart was pounding. She felt as shy as a teenager out on a first date. She felt tongue-tied.

They sat together on the sofa, simply holding hands.

'When Amber left me I felt I could never love again and I must be honest and say that falling in love with you, Kelly, wasn't like falling in love with

Amber. It was a gradual feeling, growing inside me. I just wanted to be near you, to hear your voice, but at first I didn't recognise it for what it was. Now I know beyond any doubt that I'm hopelessly in love with you.'

Despite the love she herself had felt for Michael for so long, Kelly wanted to urge him to be cautious. She wished he hadn't mentioned Amber like that because now she felt she should tell Michael that Amber had been in touch. But still she kept silent, feeling that now was not the time.

These first precious moments since declaring their love for one another should be theirs alone. Amber should not come between them. Kelly was also wondering whether she should tell Michael that she had loved him since the first day she saw him, playing tennis with Amber on that hot, sunny afternoon, so long ago.

8

During the next few weeks, Kelly and Michael spent as much time together as they could. It was a particularly exciting time for them both, not only because they had declared their love for one another, but because the plans for the updating of the health centres were gradually but definitely taking shape and soon the workmen would be moving in, followed by the decorators.

They had started to have Sunday lunch at the Hammonds' home every week and Michael suggested they use such an occasion to tell his parents about their relationship.

'Let's tell Mum and Dad today, shall we?' he said when he came to pick Kelly up to drive her to Helford.

'I thought they knew all about them,' Kelly said, thinking he meant about the health centres.

'Not about us they don't. I wanted the time to be just right and now I think it is.'

Kelly smiled.

'That's fine by me.'

But still she had moments of apprehension. She knew Mr and Mrs Hammond were very fond of her and she had not forgotten her conversation with Mrs Hammond on Christmas Day, but when she and Michael said they intended to get married, would that really be what Michael's parents wanted to hear?

Her fears were groundless. Michael made his announcement as they were having coffee in the sitting-room. He came and sat beside Kelly and took hold of her hand.

'Kelly and I have decided to get married,' he said simply.

Mrs Hammond's face shone with happiness.

'Oh, that's wonderful!' she cried and came to kiss them both. 'I'm so pleased.'

She turned to her husband.

'Isn't that wonderful, John?'

Mr Hammond beamed.

'It certainly is.'

'Of course, we haven't fixed a date yet,' Michael said. 'I've still to buy Kelly a ring.'

There was an awkward silence then. Kelly could see from Mrs Hammond's expression that Michael's mother was having the same thought that she was, remembering the day when Michael and Amber had announced their engagement, the way Amber had excitedly and proudly showed off her solitaire diamond.

I'll choose something completely different, Kelly told herself and couldn't help wondering what Michael had done with Amber's ring.

Michael went on breezily, 'It will be a summer wedding, July or August, nothing lavish. We both want a quiet affair.'

They had already discussed getting married and the type of wedding they wanted.

'Not like the wedding you'd planned with Amber, eh, son?' Mr Hammond put in jovially.

His wife rounded on him, looking embarrassed.

'John Hammond!' she scolded.

He looked suitably chastened.

'Oh, sorry, have I put my foot in it?' he mumbled.

'Not at all, Dad,' Michael said, putting his arm around Kelly's shoulders and giving them a squeeze. 'We mustn't be afraid of mentioning Amber's name, otherwise there's going to be impossible tension whenever Kelly and I talk about our own wedding and our love for one another. No way is that going to be allowed to happen. Amber is out of my life now and there is no bitterness in me towards her. There was at first, but no longer. I love Kelly and she loves me and we want the whole world to know it.'

Kelly felt overwhelmed at Michael's heartfelt speech and it was at that moment she decided it was time to come clean about Amber's visit to the house. She waited till he was driving her home later in the day.

'Michael,' she began, 'there's something I need to tell you. Something I should have told you a long time ago.'

The serious note in her voice made Michael glance at her anxiously.

'What is it?' he asked.

'Amber came to the house on Christmas Eve.'

'To your house?'

Kelly nodded.

'Yes. I'm sorry I didn't tell you sooner, but I didn't want you to be hurt.'

Michael concentrated on his driving for a few moments and Kelly feared she had upset him, perhaps not because of what she had said but because she'd kept the news from him.

Then he said, 'Was she all right?'

'She was fine. She's living in York, sharing a flat with another girl of about her own age. She's got a job, but more importantly she's going to night school to take her GCSEs, then hopefully to university.'

'I see,' Michael said. 'So she has ambitions after all. I'd always imagined Amber to be tailor-made for someone's wife and the mother of his children.'

Without warning, Michael struck the steering-wheel sharply causing Kelly to stare at him.

'Oh, no! I can't believe I said that. How trite it sounded, and so patronising. I'm sorry, Kelly. If Amber contacts you again, tell her I wish her all the best.'

'Yes, I will. I'm sorry I didn't tell you before. It was wrong of me. You had a right to know Amber had been in touch, but she didn't want you to know at the time.'

'Fair enough,' Michael said.

They didn't speak much after that and Kelly felt uncomfortable. What was Michael thinking at that moment? Had speaking of Amber stirred up old feelings? When they reached the house Michael followed Kelly silently up the drive. Inside, she removed her coat and he did the same. Then she turned to him.

'Do you want a drink?' she asked.

'No, I don't want anything, thank you. Come here.'

She moved rather slowly into his arms.

'Look at me, Kelly.'

She did so. He was smiling.

'Stop worrying your little head about your sister, do you hear me? You know what I told my parents. I'm over Amber now, completely over her. It's you I love, Kelly, with all my heart. What do I have to do to convince you?'

She allowed him to kiss her and stood resting her head against him.

'I know you love me, Michael,' she said, 'and I love you, but can I make just one other little confession and then that's that?'

Michael pretended to look horrified.

'Now what? You're not going to tell me you've been married before and have six children, are you?'

Kelly laughed.

'Nothing so terrible. It's just that I've been in love with you since the first day I met you.'

Michael took her face in both his hands and kissed her softly on the lips.

'That makes me feel both flattered and humbled,' he said simply.

It was about that time that Kelly decided a trip to York was in order. She had to tell Amber about herself and Michael and the sooner she did so the better. For the time being she did not intend to tell Michael what she had planned.

She left early on Saturday morning, when she knew Michael would be at one or the other of his centres and would more than likely be fully occupied for most of the day. Kelly had not let her sister know she was coming. If it should turn out that Amber wasn't at home, she would simply spend the day in the city.

She hadn't been to Amber's flat before and had no idea where it was so she took a taxi from the station. She had decided to travel by train to save the bother of trying to find somewhere to park.

It turned out that Amber and Holly lived in a tree-lined suburb not too far from the station and before you entered the city walls. Their flat was the top one in a converted, Victorian house, attractive and solid looking with a small but neat garden to the front. Inside, the building was clean but did not have a lift so Kelly had to climb several flights of stairs to reach the top floor. She crossed her fingers as she rang the bell.

After a few moments there came the sound of a bolt being drawn and a key being turned in the lock. Then the door opened and Amber stood there, still wearing a dressing-gown though it was by now the middle of the morning.

'Kelly!' she cried, totally surprised.

'Hello, Amber,' Kelly said.

Amber ushered her inside, pushing her hair off her face.

'I thought you were the milkman

coming for his money,' she remarked, leading Kelly along a narrow passage to a large, airy kitchen.

Kelly gave a quick glance around. She was pleased to see that all was neat and tidy and, above all, clean.

'Perhaps I should have phoned first,' she said hesitatingly.

'Oh, no, don't worry about it,' Amber reassured her. 'I'm just having my breakfast. Would you like a cup of coffee?'

'Yes, please.'

Amber went to switch on the kettle, talking as she took a mug off a hook and spooned instant coffee into it.

'I had a rather late night last night. Friday night and all that.'

She turned to grin at Kelly.

'On the town, were you?' Kelly smiled.

'Rather!'

Kelly was pleased that her sister apparently had a healthy social life. It made what she had to say so much easier.

'Where's Holly?' she asked as Amber brought her coffee.

'She's away for the weekend, visiting her parents.'

Kelly took off her coat and folded it over the back of a chair before sitting down and sipping her coffee.

'It seems a nice flat,' she remarked.

Amber returned to her half-eaten breakfast, toast and marmalade and what looked like hot chocolate.

'Yes, we're lucky. It's a very nice area. Holly makes sure I'm as domesticated as she is.'

Kelly was surprised. She knew Amber was not a lover of housework but Holly had appeared to be a very happy-go-lucky person who would hate cleaning and dusting more than Amber. But she was obviously wrong. Amber did not miss her expression.

'Yes, Kelly,' she began, 'we do own a vacuum cleaner and a couple of dusters.'

They both laughed.

'Sorry,' Kelly apologised.

It felt good to be sitting there with Amber again. There didn't seem to be any of the tension that there had been when Amber came home on Christmas Eve. How long would that happy state continue once Kelly had told Amber her news?

'How are you, Kelly?' Amber asked, suddenly becoming serious.

'I'm fine, and I can see that you are. Have you started your evening classes?'

Amber nodded, wrinkling her nose in that attractive way she had.

'It's very hard work. I'm a bit long in the tooth to be a schoolgirl.'

'Nonsense!' Kelly cried. 'People in their fifties, even sixties, go into further education these days.'

'Well, this time round I'm determined to get good grades. I've got to prove to myself that I can make something of my life. I've always envied you, Kelly, going to university, getting a law degree.'

Whilst, Kelly thought, I sometimes envied you your ability to make so many friends, to be so popular, especially with the opposite sex. She kept those thoughts to herself as Amber swallowed the last drops of her hot chocolate and took her plate and mug to the sink. Kelly got up, too, to deposit her own mug alongside Amber's.

'I'd better get dressed,' Amber said. 'Go into the living-room. I won't be long.'

She showed Kelly into the large, high-ceilinged room that overlooked the quiet avenue. There was a solid-looking three-piece suite, a long, glass-topped coffee table under the floor-to-ceiling window, a television and music centre and in one of the chimney alcoves, a pine desk. Cushions and ornaments gave the room a lived-in, comfortable look. It was warm, too, a home from home. She felt better for having seen it and knew she need have no worries about Amber being able to look after herself.

No, her only worry at the moment was about having to tell Amber she and

Michael were going to get married. As soon as Amber returned, wearing jeans and a sweater, with her long hair fastened up in a ponytail, Kelly said, 'I expect you're wondering why I've come, aren't you?'

Amber went and sat in one of the armchairs, folding her legs up underneath her.

'I thought it was purely a social call,' she said.

'Not really. Oh, don't get me wrong, I've been wanting to come and see you for a while, but I have a special reason for coming today.'

She paused.

'Yes?' Amber prompted.

Kelly looked directly into Amber's eyes.

'Michael and I have become engaged.'

Amber's eyes strayed to Kelly's left hand and she hurried on.

'We haven't bought a ring yet. Michael's been tremendously busy. He's having a lot of alterations done at his fitness centres, making them suitable for disabled people to use. He's improved so much, Amber. His limp's hardly noticeable now and he's going into hospital again in a couple of months to have plastic surgery on his face. The doctors are very hopeful his scar can be reduced, if not eliminated altogether.'

Kelly knew she was speaking much too fast but she seemed unable to stop. She only paused when Amber interrupted her.

'And you fell in love with one another, is that what you're trying to tell me? When did this happen? Were you lovers when I came home at Christmas?'

Kelly flushed.

'We're not lovers now, not in the way you mean. And no, it happened after Christmas. We suddenly realised . . . we'd been spending so much time together . . . '

'In other words, you stood by Michael whilst I did the dirty on him. I couldn't face marrying a man who was crippled and had a scar on his face, but none of that bothered you, did it, Kelly?'

Amber sounded angry, hurt, upset, vindictive even and Kelly's own anger rose to the surface.

'Yes, all right, Amber, I was a friend to Michael when he needed one most, and out of our friendship came love. And I'm not ashamed. I know I can make him very happy.'

'Which is more than I would have done,' Amber snapped back.

'Oh, Amber, why are we fighting like this? You gave Michael up. You didn't want to marry him. It's taken him a long time to start to re-build, not only his life, but also his confidence.'

Kelly was thinking, should she tell Amber the truth, about how she had always loved Michael ever since Amber first met him? She decided that doing so would only make matters worse and would serve no useful purpose. But she had to ask, and she did so in a very small voice.

'Do you still love him, Amber?'

Kelly waited with held breath for Amber's answer.

'No,' Amber said at last. 'There would be no place for Michael in my life. I sometimes wonder if I ever loved him really. Perhaps it was infatuation, puppy love. At any rate, when it came to the test, I was weighed in the balance and found wanting.'

She suddenly smiled but Kelly did not miss the sparkle of tears in her sister's eyes.

'You and Michael are much more suited to one another than he and I ever were.'

'Are we really? But I'm not the outdoor type and hopeless at sports.'

Why was she running herself down like that?

'There's more to love and marriage than being able to play badminton,' Amber said.

She came and sat by Kelly on the sofa.

'I'm so happy for you, Kelly, really I am. Michael's a very lucky man. I only wish I could undo some of the hurt I did him.'

'Michael bears no grudges,' Kelly said.

Amber hugged her.

'I'm sorry I reacted the way I did. It was a shock, I suppose, but I'm getting used to the idea now and I'm happy for you both. I truly am.'

Kelly returned her sister's fierce hug, feeling a tremendous sense of relief that it had all been said at last. Now she could go back to Michael and look forward to the rest of their lives together.

9

The Mayor and Mayoress of Helford, wearing their chains of office, officially opened the newly-furbished and newly-named health and fitness centres on a fine, sunny morning in early May, travelling from Peppermint Place to Cinnamon Place in their official limousine.

When the ribbon at the second centre had been cut, champagne and light refreshments were offered to the invited guests, which included representatives from various organisations.

Kelly, keeping in the background, watched Michael circulating. Her heart swelled with love for him. He looked so handsome in his light grey suit, white shirt and dark tie. Kelly looked down at her hand, caressing the engagement ring that Michael had placed there some weeks before. Plans for their

wedding were going ahead, and she had
never been happier. Michael caught her
eye and smiled, saying something to
Philip, the young architect, before
crossing to Kelly's side.

'This is a great day, isn't it?' Michael
said, putting his arm around Kelly's
shoulders.

'I'm so proud of you, Michael,' Kelly
said, 'and of Philip, of course.'

'Yes.'

Michael glanced at the young architect chatting now to the mayor.

'He's certainly a man of vision. He
fully intends to be the first client in the
new pool.'

Kelly looked around the large area,
taking in the gym equipment, some of
it new. There was also an area of toning
tables, an air-conditioned exercise
room, a sauna and showers. The new
decor of cinnamon and white added an
elegant, relaxing touch. Where before
there had been any steps now ramps
were also in place. Doors had been
widened for wheel-chair access, and it

was all very impressive.

As Michael's claim for compensation against the driver who had maimed him was still on-going, he had managed to fund everything himself, with the aid of a grant from the local authority, hence the mayor's and mayoress's presence and participation in today's opening ceremonies.

Michael gave Kelly a light kiss on the cheek.

'Of course, I intend to enrol you here as a new member,' he said.

Kelly shook her head, laughing.

'Oh, no!' she cried.

'Oh, yes,' Michael returned. 'A little light exercise is good for you. We have an excellent ladies-only section. And don't make the excuse you haven't any proper gear to wear or no decent trainers. I sell both.'

Kelly groaned.

'You're a slave driver,' she protested.

But she didn't mind, in fact she had been thinking about coming along to the centre and making the effort. She wanted to back Michael all the way, to share in the things that were dear to his heart. She had spent her life so far standing on the sidelines, being merely an onlooker. She vowed that would change.

Eventually all the guests had departed and Kelly and Michael were the only ones remaining. Caterers had been on hand to serve the drinks and refreshments, but they, too, had finished clearing up and gone on their way. Everywhere seemed very quiet after the hum of conversation and the sound of happy laughter had ended. Michael sat down on one of the high stools at the soft drinks' bar.

'Gosh, I'm whacked,' he exclaimed.

Immediately Kelly was concerned. She went over to him, putting her arms around him, resting her head against his shoulder.

'You've been overdoing it,' she admonished him gently.

He took hold of her hand and patted her fingers.

'Possibly,' he agreed, 'but hasn't it all been worth it? I keep thinking what I was like after the accident, especially after Amber left me. I didn't think I had anything left to live for. Now I've got my centres and I know I'll be helping other people who are more physically disabled than I ever was. But, most of all, Kelly, I've got you.'

He kissed her.

'Thank you for standing by me and having faith in me.'

Foolishly Kelly felt tears pricking the back of her eyes. She gave Michael a fierce hug.

'I love you so much, Michael,' was all she could think of to say.

'By the way,' Michael said and felt in his jacket pocket, to produce a narrow, buff-coloured envelope. 'This arrived this morning.'

'What is it?'

But she knew what it was. She recognised the envelope and the franked lettering near the stamp. It was from the hospital. It could only be to do with Michael's operation.

'I've to go into hospital on the sixteenth,' Michael said solemnly.

So soon — less than two weeks away! Kelly felt a cold hand of dread clutch at her stomach. Seeing her expression, Michael gave her a little shake.

'Now, none of that,' he scolded. 'I'll be fine. I have the utmost confidence in Mr Petersen.'

Kelly traced her finger along the length of Michael's scar.

'I almost love it,' she murmured.

Michael gave a short laugh.

'I wouldn't so as far as to say that, but I suppose I have sort of got used to having it around,' he admitted.

'Do you know how long you'll be in hospital?' Kelly asked.

'About a week, I think.'

Kelly hid her shock. Oh, she knew a week wasn't long, but once Michael had gone into hospital she knew that every minute she spent apart from him would seem like a year. She was being silly because during their every-day life they spent much of their time apart, but it would be so different, knowing Michael was undergoing a delicate operation, then the agonising wait till the bandages were removed. It would be like reliving those nightmarish days after his accident.

Michael got up from the stool.

'Let's go get something to eat,' he said cheerfully.

'We've been nibbling most of the afternoon,' Kelly reminded him.

'Nibbling, yes, but not eating,' Michael said. 'We'll walk round to our favourite Italian and leave the car here. I've had two glasses of champagne and I intend to drink wine with my meal, so definitely, no driving. And no talk about my operation. That's an order!'

She would comply, but Kelly knew that nothing Michael could say would be able to keep thoughts of what lay ahead from her mind.

The following Thursday, Kelly spent most of the day in Leeds at the magistrates' court, returning home about half past three in the afternoon. It was another lovely day, the weather mild and sunny. As the evenings were very light now Kelly decided once she had showered, changed and had something to eat she would go round to Michael's and suggest they go for a walk. It was one type of exercise that Kelly didn't mind taking and Michael found that walking was good for his leg, though his limp was practically non-existent these days.

Having decided to walk there, it was about half-past six when Kelly finally reached the bungalow on Elm Avenue.

As she turned the corner into the avenue, she noticed the red car parked in Michael's drive. She was sure it didn't belong to anybody she knew. It looked very new and as she got nearer, Kelly saw, by the registration, that it was indeed only a couple of years old.

Feeling curious, she walked up the drive and fitted her key in the front door. Michael had given her a key some time ago, when she also had given him a key to her house. As she entered the hall she was about to call out when she heard voices and laughter coming from the direction of the kitchen.

It quickly became apparent that Michael's visitor was female. Kelly's curiosity increased. She walked along the hallway towards the half-open kitchen door. Then she heard a woman's voice and she knew at once — it was Amber!

Amber was here — but why? She must have passed her driving test and bought herself a car, but what was she doing at Michael's house? Why hadn't she been home first? With tension now mingling with her curiosity Kelly stood awkwardly outside the kitchen door, knowing Michael and Amber would be totally unaware of her existence. She hated herself for eavesdropping but felt compelled to do so.

'Oh, Michael,' Amber was saying, 'you don't know how it feels to be with you again after all this time.'

She sounded blissfully happy.

When Kelly heard Michael say, 'Me, too, You look wonderful, Amber. You've grown up.'

'So you thought I was just a child before?'

Amber's voice was teasing now.

'In some ways, yes, but not any more.'

'No, not any more,' Amber agreed. 'I suppose Kelly will have to know. I was going to phone her but I didn't want to tell her over the phone. Now, I think that might be the best way, don't you? I don't know what she's going to think of me.'

'And me. If she thinks we're sharing a secret she mightn't like it. Why don't you phone her now? Ask her if it's OK to go round there?'

'Should I?'

Amber didn't sound too certain.

'Of course. No point in putting it off.'

'OK, I will.'

Kelly heard the scraping of chair legs on the tiled floor and stood with her heart in her mouth waiting to be discovered when Amber came out into the hall to use the phone, but when she heard Amber saying, 'There doesn't seem to be any reply,' she realised her sister was using the wall phone in the kitchen.

She wanted to run away. She didn't want to hear any more, but somehow she was rooted to the spot.

'She's been to Leeds,' Michael said. 'We'll go round later, give her a chance to get home. Shall I take you to one of the clubs, Amber? Would you like to see what we've done there?'

'Oh, yes, I would.'

'I don't know what I would have done without Kelly.'

Michael's voice was low and serious.

'Oh, Michael,' Kelly heard Amber saying. 'I know I hurt you and I'm so sorry, but let's think about the future, shall we? Both our futures. I'm so excited. I know what's happening is the right thing for all of us.'

'So do I, angel.'

There was a pause, perhaps only a moment in time but to Kelly it seemed like an eternity. Were Amber and Michael in each other's arms? Were they kissing? He had called her angel, his old name for her. Amber had come back to claim Michael and it was obvious that he wasn't putting up much resistance.

He must still love her and was willing to forgive the way she had treated him. Kelly cursed herself for the way she had kept going on at Amber that day in York when she told how much improved Michael was; how he was going to have more surgery on his facial scar. Kelly remembered, too, how jealous Amber had sounded at first when she heard Kelly and Michael had become engaged. Did she really still love Michael or was it only that she couldn't bear Kelly to have him?

Whatever the true situation was, it was obvious that Michael still loved Amber, that he had never stopped loving her. She, Kelly, had merely been a substitute, someone to tend his wounds and soothe his pain. She had just heard him tell Amber he didn't know what he would have done without Kelly. She had been in the right place, at the right time, that was all.

Her eyes filled with bitter, angry tears and she dashed them away with the back of her hand.

When she heard Michael saying, 'I want things to be just as they used to be, Amber. After we're married I hope we can all stay good friends.'

'We will, Michael, don't worry,' Amber answered. 'As you said, I'm all grown up now. I shall be a loyal and true wife. There's to be no running away ever again, I promise.'

Kelly waited to hear no more. She had to get away before Michael and Amber made a move out of the kitchen. She opened the door quietly and ran down the drive, turning towards the end of the avenue, running all the way back home. She arrived there sobbing and out of breath, letting herself into the house, standing with her back against the door.

She was shaking; she didn't know what to do. What if Michael and Amber should come round here? They had made it plain they wanted her to know about them as soon as possible. Could Michael really be so callous he could turn up on the doorstep with Amber and calmly announce they had got back together again? Kelly knew she couldn't be there if they did.

She didn't want to hear what either of them had to say. She couldn't trust herself to be there. She needed time to herself, to come to terms with what she had overheard, to try to put an innocent explanation on to it, but she knew there wasn't one.

Amber had decided she still wanted Michael. Perhaps she had realised she had acted too hastily when she left him like she had. Unable to face life with a less than perfect man she had fled, but Michael was healing, something Amber had never paused to consider.

And Michael? He had stated many times that he no longer loved Amber, that he was completely over her but had he merely been trying to convince himself that this was so? Now Amber had gone back to him, begging his forgiveness no doubt, and because of the strong love he still had for her, Michael had succumbed.

Kelly moved away from the door. She felt used, hurt and angry. She wished she had had the strength to face the pair of them, stood her ground but instead she had run away. And coming back home like this wasn't running away far enough.

Without hesitation, Kelly ran upstairs and quickly packed a large hold-all, the one she used when she had to stay away overnight should she be attending court in another town. She filled her toilet bag and made sure she had her credit card and that her wallet had sufficient cash. She didn't stop to consider where she was going or what she was going to do about going to the office the next morning. She thought about nothing except getting away, as far away from Michael and Amber as she could go.

She locked up the house, making sure all the windows were closed and went out to her car. She deliberately drove in the direction that would not necessitate her going anywhere near Elm Avenue.

10

In the end, Kelly did not go so far from home. Skirting the outer areas of Helford, she saw the familiar white painted Red Lion Inn where she and Michael had had the occasional drink. Kelly knew they did bed and breakfast as well as hearty, appetising bar meals and almost automatically she pulled into the carpark.

Within a very short while she was settled in a single, comfortable bedroom, overlooking the fields at the rear of the inn. She sat in the small armchair near the bed, staring at her luggage, wondering what on earth she was doing there.

This could only be a temporary resting place till she came to terms with what she had overheard at Michael's house. Her problems were not going to disappear no matter how long she hid herself away. Sooner or later she was going to have to face Michael and Amber. But she couldn't do it yet. She was too shocked, too hurt. She stood up and went over to the washbasin to pour herself a glass of water, gulping it down in one desperate swallow.

Because she was still in Helford there was always going to be the possibility of her and Michael coming across one another, but she didn't intend to stay at the Red Lion for long, a couple of nights at the most. The first thing she must do was to phone someone from the office to make some excuse for not going in there the next day.

Luckily there was a phone in the room and Kelly waited for an outside line before dialling. Tim Collins, her immediate superior, answered the phone on the third ring.

Kelly had to use all her strength to stop breaking down then and there. Tim was in his fifties, a devoted family man, who had always had a fatherly manner towards Kelly. She could imagine him standing by his phone, an evening paper under his arm perhaps, his glasses, as always, on the end of his nose.

'Tim,' she began, 'I'm sorry to phone you at home like this.'

'That's all right. Is anything wrong?'

'No, not really, but I won't be in to work for a couple of days. Some personal business. I'll explain later. Will that be all right?'

'Of course. No problem, Kelly. Anything I can help with?'

'No, thanks. I've got to go now. I'll be in touch as soon as I can.'

They said goodbye and Kelly went to take her night things and toilet bag from her case. She left the other items in there. To hang clothes in the wardrobe would have seemed too much like an admission of permanence. She toyed with the idea of going down to the bar, but decided against it. Not because she thought Michael might come in, she knew it wasn't one of his regular watering holes, but rather because she didn't want to be with other people just then.

Would Michael and Amber have left the health centre by now? Would they have tried to phone her again, or gone to the house? Would Michael be worried about her continuing absence or would he see it as a reprieve, a delay in the time he would have to make his confession?

Kelly sat in the chair going over and over in her mind what she had overheard. Neither Amber nor Michael, she realised, had sounded in any way guilty or as if they dreaded having to face her, but surely they must. They had talked about getting married. They must realise that Michael had a responsibility towards Kelly. She was wearing the ring he had given her, a token of his promise to marry her.

Staring at her left hand through tear-filled eyes, Kelly didn't know how she was going to get through the night. It would be worse, so much worse, to lose Michael now than if he had never been hers. How could she go on seeing him and Amber together again? And what of Mr and Mrs Hammond? Wouldn't they be hurt and shocked, too? They had never actually reproached Amber because of her treatment of their only son, but Kelly knew feelings had run deep. Could Michael really expect them to kiss and make up as easily as he had done?

She began to wonder if Michael and Amber had any idea what they had started because of this renewed devotion to one another. She removed the ring from her finger and put it in the zip compartment of her shoulder bag. And then, because she could suddenly not stand being on her own a moment longer, she slipped the strap of her bag over her shoulder and headed downstairs to the cosy, comfortable bar where at this time in the evening there was only a handful of people.

Kelly went to the bar and asked for a slimline tonic. The bartender, who was also the landlord, tried to make polite conversation with her.

'Room all right?' he began.

'Yes, fine, thank you,' Kelly said.

'Just passing through, are you?'

She nodded.

The landlord pressed on.

'You seem familiar. Have you stayed here before?'

Kelly smiled.

'No, I haven't.'

The landlord grinned, setting her glass down on the bar.

'Been in the bar before then?'

'No.'

That wasn't strictly true but Kelly didn't want to answer any more questions, however friendly they were. She paid for the drink and took it as far away from the bar as she could get, sitting at a small, round table very near to where a lone young man was hunched over an untouched drink. He looked up at her briefly but didn't smile or speak. He did, however, pick up his glass and take a drink as though just realising it was there. Then he set it down on the table again and left it.

Kelly sipped her own drink. She looked around, more for something to do than because she was interested in what she was seeing. Another couple had entered the pub and were busy studying the bar menu. The young man in the corner was now staring straight ahead of him, as though in a kind of daze. He looked sad, in fact he had one of the saddest faces Kelly had ever seen. Was he always like that, or like her, had something happened to him to make him unhappy?

He was wearing a brown T-shirt and he also wore glasses, narrow, metal-framed ones that gave this young man an old-fashioned, even quaint appearance. When he placed his hands, slowly and carefully, on top of the table, on either side of his glass and seemed to sit staring at them, Kelly noticed how long and slender his fingers were and was convinced he was an artist or a sculptor.

Suddenly, he glanced at her and she

hurriedly looked away, picking up her own glass again and taking a long drink. She hoped he didn't think she was angling for him to make conversation. That was the last thing she was interested in. She couldn't understand why she found him so fascinating. She wasn't the type of person who would normally sit on her own in a public house and do a character study of a complete stranger.

She knew, of course, she was only trying to keep her mind occupied, to keep her from dwelling on Michael and Amber, thinking about what they were doing and beginning to realise she had acted very hastily in running away as she had done. She should have stayed and faced them. She should have pushed open the kitchen door and confronted them. If she had only done that, by now it would all be out in the open. As it was she had merely put off the inevitable.

She saw the landlord coming round from behind the bar and he seemed to be walking straight towards her. She steeled herself for further, unwanted conversation, but he merely nodded to her and went instead to the young man's table.

'The wife says you're wanting a local bus timetable,' he said.

'Yes, please, I do.'

For the first time, the young man smiled and his sad face suddenly became the most pleasant and friendly face you could imagine.

'Right. I'll let you have one before you go up to your room.'

'Thank you very much.'

The landlord gave a thumbs-up gesture and went back behind the bar. The young man took another drink from his glass, this time a long one, wiping the froth from his mouth with the back of his hand. Once again he gave Kelly a sharp, unexpected glance and once again she swiftly averted her own gaze. This time, however, the man moved along the padded bench nearer to her table, bringing his glass with him.

Oh, no, Kelly thought!

'Excuse me, but do I know you?'

Here goes, it's a come-on, Kelly groaned.

'No, I don't think so,' she said politely but also she hoped in the sort of voice that would stop him in his tracks.

'Your face, it's very familiar. I never forget a face.'

'That makes two of you,' Kelly gave him a cold look.

'Sorry?'

'The landlord thought I looked familiar as well, but I can assure you I don't know either of you.'

The young man gave another of his friendly smiles.

'It'll come to me suddenly,' he said cheerfully.

Kelly got to her feet abruptly.

'Excuse me,' she murmured.

He rose, too.

'Look, I'm not trying to pick you up, honestly I'm not,' he assured her. 'And

I wasn't just shooting you a line. I have seen your face before, I just know I have.'

He seemed so sincere a young man, so earnest that Kelly found herself relenting a little.

'You must admit it's a bit corny,' she said.

He shrugged his shoulders.

'Yes, I know, but I shall probably spend the rest of my stay here wracking my brains. Are you a resident, by any chance?'

'How did you guess?'

'Probably because you're a woman here alone, and that's unusual.'

'Yes, I'm staying here, for a night or two.'

'Me, too. My name's James Reid.'

He offered her his hand. Kelly hesitated. This could still be a come-on and if it was she wanted no part in it, but on the other hand, if they were going to have to face each other at breakfast the next morning they couldn't really avoid contact, could they?

She took hold of the young man's fingers.

'How do you do,' she said.

He put his head to one side.

'So I take it you don't want me to know your name. Fair enough. Will you let me buy you a drink then?'

'Well, I was going to go out and get some fresh air. I'm finding it a bit stuffy in here.'

This was true, as more and more people came into the bar, some smoking. The atmosphere was becoming distinctly fuggy.

'Good idea.'

With his hand beneath her elbow, James Reid guided her through the throng towards the open door, in such a manner that, without making a scene, Kelly could not stop him. She was faintly surprised, after the rather gloomy interior, when she saw that the sun was still shining brilliantly outside and her watch told her that it was only half past eight.

They strolled across the carpark

towards the small beer garden and children's play area. Both were deserted and Kelly sat down on a bench, lifting her face to the soft, warm rays of the evening sun. James Reid sat next to her.

'You looked very unhappy in there,' he remarked casually.

She looked at him.

'I could say the same about you.'

Now, they had both confessed that each had been watching the other. The knowledge made Kelly feel a little embarrassed. James gave a brief smile, then removed his glasses and carefully polished them with a clean, white handkerchief before replacing them. Then he spoke.

'Yes, well, perhaps I have cause to be. Unhappy that is.'

Was he waiting for her to ask why, Kelly wondered. She did not really want to act as confessor to this young man. She had troubles enough of her own and certainly she did not intend sharing hers with him.

Without waiting for her to say

anything at all, he went on, 'I keep telling myself not to be so stupid. 'Wait', my girlfriend told me. 'This is something I have to do.' So I waited. Not very long, I admit. Then I panicked and came here. I know my girl won't be very pleased when she finds out, if she finds out. I know I should go back home and not let her discover I followed her, but I can't. It's not that I don't trust her . . . '

His voice trailed off.

So, Kelly thought, James Reid, like herself, was in love with someone who possibly did not love him enough in return. Strangely, she wished she could think of something comforting, encouraging to say to him, but she couldn't.

He was speaking again.

'I haven't known her long but I love her so much. I asked her to marry me on our third meeting, but she's the cautious type. We have to get to know one another, she says. We're both students and we've got to complete our studies. She keeps reminding me that if we've got our whole lives to spend together, there's no need to rush headlong into anything. And then, there's this compulsion of hers. She hasn't kept anything from me, I know that, and I also know she's right in what she's doing, but I can't help being scared, because of what she has told me.'

To Kelly, he was speaking in riddles and she really didn't want to hear any more. He had her sympathy, but knowing what she herself still had to face, she was in no mood to let James Reid weep on her shoulder. But how could she get away from him without appearing rude and heartless?

She started to speak before he could get launched again, choosing her words carefully.

'Look . . . James . . . I don't think you should be telling me all this. It's something that should concern only yourself and your girlfriend.'

To her surprise, he agreed with her immediately.

'Yes, you're right,' he said. 'And I apologise. Why should you have to put up with the moanings of a lovesick stranger? Forgive me and let me buy you a drink, please.'

He stood up.

'And I promise not to go on about myself. I'll let you talk about yourself instead.'

Kelly laughed and also stood up.

'We'll discuss the weather or something harmless like that, shall we?'

The smile returned to his face.

'All right, but will you at least tell me your name now? I never talk about the weather with someone I haven't been properly introduced to.'

Kelly held out her hand easily. She liked James Reid and she believed they could have a conversation that wouldn't hold any pitfalls for either one of them.

'I'm Kelly,' she said simply.

James shook hands with her for the second time. His grip was firm and strong. Then as they started walking back towards the inn he stopped abruptly.

'Kelly?'

His brow creased.

'That's my name!' Kelly said, laughing.

Understanding seemed to dawn on his face.

'Of course! I knew I'd seen you before somewhere. My word, what a coincidence. You're Amber's sister!'

Kelly froze.

'You know Amber?' she asked in a small voice.

'Of course I know her. She's my girl, and she has a photograph of you and her together in her flat. That's why I thought your face seemed so familiar.'

Kelly felt confused. How on earth was she going to be able to tell James that the girl he loved so much had gone back to her former fiancé? This was the only thought that occupied her mind at that moment.

'I feel such a fool,' James went on. 'Now you know who I am and I know who you are, I'm sure you must be aware why Amber's come back here. She said she would be going to see you straight after she'd seen Michael. Did she turn up?'

'No . . . er . . . no, she didn't.'

Kelly started walking back to the pub again and James fell into step beside her. Kelly's head was buzzing. She was trying to think what she had overheard in Michael's house. Had she misunderstood? Had she put two and two together and come up with the wrong answer?

'Well, she certainly intends to see you. She was going to phone me from your house later. Of course, I'm here now so that won't be any good, will it? Damn, I've made a real mess of things. I say, you won't tell Amber about our meeting, will you? I've made up my mind to go back to York and not stay here tonight. I intended going along to your village in the morning, but I can see now that if I do I'm going to make Amber one very cross girl. She'll probably be hurt, too, and think I don't trust her and I do.'

Kelly thought it was time she did some talking for a change.

'Look,' she began, 'let's get inside the pub and sit down. I've got something to tell you now. After that we can decide what to do.'

James didn't argue.

'Lead the way,' he said.

11

Kelly told James everything, about Michael's accident, Amber's leaving him and how she and Michael had themselves fallen in love and planned to marry. She explained how she had gone to Michael's house and overheard him and Amber talking.

She found it so easy to talk to James, as though she had known him a long time, and talking like that had a curious, calming effect on her. For the first time since she had listened at the kitchen door she felt a faint stirring of hope, a lifting of her gloom. If James was right and Amber loved him and not Michael then she, Kelly, had made a dreadful mistake but nothing that couldn't be put right so long as she acted quickly. The amazing coincidence of meeting James had given her the chance to put things right and she had to act upon it right away.

When her story was told James smiled at her.

'You're so wrong about Amber and Michael,' he said. 'Oh, I know they were engaged and I know that Amber let Michael down badly. She's told me all that and she feels very bad about herself. That's why she felt she had to go to Michael, don't you see, and tell him how sorry she was for the way she treated him. Only then, she said, could there be any future for us. Your sister has grown up this last twelve months, Kelly. I know we're both young, I know Amber has been in love before, but I'm willing to put my trust in her because I love her. Can you do the same? And Michael? Can't you trust him, too?'

'Yes, I do trust him, honestly I do, but when I heard them speaking, it sounded so . . . '

She couldn't put it into words.

James touched her hand lightly.

'I know. You don't have to explain anything to me, Kelly.'

'If I go back home now do you think it'll be too late? They were going to the gym. I don't know how long they intended staying there,' she said, glancing nervously at her watch.

It was almost nine o'clock.

'You have to go back. What else can you do? Can't you make some excuse?' James replied.

'I won't lie, James,' Kelly said firmly. 'Neither of us must lie.'

'No, of course not, but I won't have to because Amber won't be home till tomorrow at the earliest. She said she would phone me if she decided to stay a few days with you. I've finally made up my mind, as it's so late, that I'll stay here. It would look bad if we both cancelled our rooms this late in the day, and I don't suppose there'd be a train to York now, anyway. But you must go back home, now, and keep your fingers crossed that you haven't been missed yet.'

She would certainly do that but she didn't hold out much hope. She felt sure Amber or Michael would have phoned her before now, or gone round to the house. They would probably be getting a bit worried about her by now. Still, there was nothing else for it. If the worst came to the worst she would have to make a full confession, however terrible that made her seem, but there would be no need to implicate James.

She had a feeling that Amber would be telling her all about James before very long. When that happened, Kelly felt certain she could carry it off and pretend innocence. Not exactly the truth, she knew that, but not lying either and it would save anyone getting hurt.

'What would have happened, James,' she asked seriously, 'if you and I hadn't met here tonight? It must be fate.'

'Perhaps it is,' James said. 'But don't let's push our luck now. You get off home and I'll be safely back in York before Amber phones me.'

Kelly smiled.

'And when Amber finally introduces

us we'll shake hands politely and say, 'How do you do'!'

James grinned.

'Something like that.'

Impulsively he bent forward and kissed her cheek.

'Good luck,' he said.

Kelly glanced up at the bar where the landlord was chatting to one of his customers. First she had to tell him she wouldn't be using the room after all and she hoped he would accept full payment for the room and her sincere apologies and leave it at that.

12

There was no car in the drive when Kelly got back home. She crept into the house as though she was an intruder, her guilty conscience weighing heavily on her. She took her bag upstairs, and remembered to replace her engagement ring, trying not to dwell on how disloyal she felt towards Michael because she had removed it. She then went to put the kettle on. It was at that moment that the telephone rang, causing her to jump. She let the phone ring several times before she went to answer it.

'Hello?' she said.

'Kelly? It's me, Michael. Have you tried to phone me this evening, darling?'

'No, no, I haven't.'

Well, that at least was true.

'Oh, good. I wouldn't have wanted you to be worried about me. I meant to contact you earlier but I had a visitor, a surprise visitor and you'll never guess who.'

'Tell me.'

Kelly felt a sharp twinge of conscience. Oh, please, she prayed, don't let me have to tell any lies.

'Your sister, Amber. I'm bringing her round there now, though she's got her own car, you know. We went to the gym and we met Karl and Carol. I haven't seen them for ages. I took them inside and they insisted on using the new pool, and then they persuaded Amber and me to go back to their place for a bite of supper. Well, to cut a long story short, we got talking. You know how it is and I suddenly realised I hadn't phoned you, so here I am. Amber's got some news for you. She can't wait to tell you. And, by the way, we're friends again. Isn't that good?'

'It's wonderful!' Kelly said. 'Oh, Michael, do hurry round here. I miss you so terribly.'

'Love you,' he said.

'I love you, too,' she returned.

She replaced the receiver. She found she was crying. Oh, she didn't deserve to be so lucky. But she still felt slightly uneasy, as though she was deceiving Michael in some way. Well, wasn't she? She made up her mind there and then that she would tell him the truth — one day. She gave a little smile. Perhaps on their Golden Wedding day, she decided.

She made the tea and got out the biscuits and when she heard Michael's car in the drive she ran out to meet him, throwing her arms around his neck, hugging him so tightly that he cried out.

Then Kelly gave Amber a fierce hug, too.

'How lovely to see you,' she said.

'From now on you'll see lots of me,' Amber promised. 'I've made my peace with Michael so there's no need for me to hide myself away.'

'There wasn't before,' Kelly told her, taking Michael and Amber into the sitting-room.

'Perhaps not,' Amber said wistfully.

Kelly perched on the arm of Amber's chair.

'So, what's this news you've got for me then?'

As if she didn't know!

Whilst Amber went on at some length extolling James Reid's virtues, her eyes bright and shining, Kelly sat by Michael with his arm around her. Occasionally she stole him a glance, aching with love for him, thinking about their future together.

Soon, Michael would go into hospital for further surgery. She would be there at his side the whole way through, and Amber, too. Now Amber could be involved. No more separation, no more tension. They could be a family again, which is what Kelly had always wanted.

We do hope that you have enjoyed reading this large print book.

Did you know that all of our titles are available for purchase?

We publish a wide range of high quality large print books including:
Romances, Mysteries, Classics
General Fiction
Non Fiction and Westerns

Special interest titles available in large print are:
The Little Oxford Dictionary
Music Book, Song Book
Hymn Book, Service Book

Also available from us courtesy of Oxford University Press:
Young Readers' Dictionary
(large print edition)
Young Readers' Thesaurus
(large print edition)

For further information or a free brochure, please contact us at:
Ulverscroft Large Print Books Ltd.,
The Green, Bradgate Road, Anstey,
Leicester, LE7 7FU, England.
Tel: (00 44) **0116 236 4325**
Fax: (00 44) **0116 234 0205**

Other titles in the
Linford Romance Library:

CONVALESCENT HEART

Lynne Collins

They called Romily the Snow Queen, but once she had been all fire and passion, kindled into loving by a man's kiss and sure it would last a lifetime. She still believed it would, for her. It had lasted only a few months for the man who had stormed into her heart. After Greg, how could she trust any man again? So was it likely that surgeon Jake Conway could pierce the icy armour that the lovely ward sister had wrapped about her emotions?

TOO MANY LOVES

Juliet Gray

Justin Caldwell, a famous personality of stage and screen, was blessed with good looks and charm that few women could resist. Stacy was a newcomer to England and she was not impressed by the handsome stranger; she thought him arrogant, ill-mannered and detestable. By the time that Justin desired to begin again on a new footing it was much too late to redeem himself in her eyes, for there had been too many loves in his life.

MYSTERY AT MELBECK

Gillian Kaye

Meg Bowering goes to Melbeck House in the Yorkshire Dales to nurse the rich, elderly Mrs Peacock. She likes her patient and is immediately attracted to Mrs Peacock's nephew and heir, Geoffrey, who farms nearby. But Geoffrey is a gambling man and Meg could never have foreseen the dreadful chain of events which follow. Throughout her ordeal, she is helped by the local vicar, Andrew Sheratt, and she soon discovers where her heart really lies.